NANCY KRESS

Winner of the

Nebula Award

Hugo Award

John W. Campbell Memorial Award

Sturgeon Award

Locus Award

Asimov Readers' Award

"Nancy Kress is one of the best science-fiction writers working today. Her use of science is tricky and thought-provoking, her command of fiction sharp and full of feeling."
—Kim Stanley Robinson, author of the *Mars* trilogy

"Nancy Kress comprehends the grimy relationships among bioscience, technology, and politics; and soon we will too, if only enough of us read her. Too soon it cannot be."
—Gene Wolfe, author of *The Book of the New Sun*

"Kress's villains are not diabolical conspirators but willfully ignorant hypocrites, shortsighted and greedy dunderheads, the well-intentioned half-baked—in short, us. But we are also the heroes whose generosity, honesty and energy could turn our lemming tribe away from the polluted waters ahead."
—*Washington Post*

"Kress's depiction of science is much like her characters' experiences with love: by turns glorious and terrible, and always a little disturbing, even in triumph."
—*Publishers Weekly*

"Her style is devilishly inventive."
—CNN.com

T0402900

Not What I Intended

PM PRESS OUTSPOKEN AUTHORS SERIES

1. *The Left Left Behind*
   Terry Bisson
2. *The Lucky Strike*
   Kim Stanley Robinson
3. *The Underbelly*
   Gary Phillips
4. *Mammoths of the Great Plains*
   Eleanor Arnason
5. *Modem Times 2.0*
   Michael Moorcock
6. *The Wild Girls*
   Ursula K. Le Guin
7. *Surfing the Gnarl*
   Rudy Rucker
8. *The Great Big Beautiful Tomorrow*
   Cory Doctorow
9. *Report from Planet Midnight*
   Nalo Hopkinson
10. *The Human Front*
    Ken MacLeod
11. *New Taboos*
    John Shirley
12. *The Science of Herself*
    Karen Joy Fowler
13. *Raising Hell*
    Norman Spinrad
14. *Patty Hearst & The Twinkie Murders: A Tale of Two Trials*
    Paul Krassner
15. *My Life, My Body*
    Marge Piercy
16. *Gypsy*
    Carter Scholz
17. *Miracles Ain't What They Used to Be*
    Joe R. Lansdale
18. *Fire.*
    Elizabeth Hand
19. *Totalitopia*
    John Crowley
20. *The Atheist in the Attic*
    Samuel R. Delany
21. *Thoreau's Microscope*
    Michael Blumlein
22. *The Beatrix Gates*
    Rachel Pollack
23. *A City Made of Words*
    Paul Park
24. *Talk like a Man*
    Nisi Shawl
25. *Big Girl*
    Meg Elison
26. *The Planetbreaker's Son*
    Nick Mamatas
27. *The First Law of Thermodynamics*
    James Patrick Kelly
28. *Utopias of the Third Kind*
    Vandana Singh
29. *Night Shift*
    Eileen Gunn
30. *The Collapsing Frontier*
    Jonathan Lethem

Not What I Intended

plus

Patent Infringement

plus

Machine Learning

and much more

Nancy Kress

PM PRESS | 2025

"Patent Infringement," was originally published in *Isaac Asimov's Science Fiction* 26, no. 5, May 2002.
"Laws of Survival," was originally published in *Jim Baen's Universe 2*, no. 4, December 2007.
"Machine Learning" was originally published in *Future Visions: Original Science Fiction Inspired by Microsoft* (Microsoft, 2015).
"Not What I Intended" and "Amy Lowell, Cixin Liu, Jane Austen, and the Art of Fiction" are original to this volume.

Not What I Intended
Nancy Kress © 2025
This edition © PM Press

ISBN (paperback): 979-8-88744-120-7
ISBN (e-book): 979-8-88744-125-2
LCCN: 2025931313

Series editors: Nick Mamatas and Nisi Shawl
Cover design by John Yates/www.stealworks.com
Author photo by Mary Grace Long
Insides by Jonathan Rowland

10 9 8 7 6 5 4 3 2 1

Printed in the USA

CONTENTS

Patent Infringement

PRESS RELEASE

Kegelman-Ballston Corporation is proud to announce the first public release of its new drug, Halitex, which cures Ulbarton's Flu completely after one ten-pill course of treatment. Ulbarton's Flu, as the public knows all too well, now afflicts upwards of thirty million Americans, with the number growing daily as the highly contagious flu spreads. Halitex "flu-proofs" the body by inserting genes tailored to confer immunity to this persistent and debilitating scourge, the symptoms of which include coughing, muscle aches, and fatigue. Because the virus remains in the body even after symptoms disappear, Ulbarton's Flu can recur in a given patient at any time. Halitex renders each recurrence ineffectual.

The General Accounting Office estimates the Ulbarton's Flu, the virus of which was first identified by Dr. Timothy Ulbarton, has already cost four billion dollars this calendar year in medical costs and lost work time. Halitex, two years in development by Kegelman-Ballston, is expected to be in high demand throughout the nation.

* * *

NEW YORK POST

K-B ZAPS ULBARTON'S FLU

NEW DRUG DOES U'S FLU 4 U

* * *

Jonathan Meese
538 Pleasant Lane
Aspen Hill, MD 20906

Dear Mr. Kegelman and Mr. Ballston,

I read in the newspaper that your company, Kegelman-Ballston, has recently released a drug, Halitex, that provides immunity against Ulbarton's Flu by gene therapy. I believe that the genes used in developing this drug are mine. Two years ago, on May 5, I visited my GP to explain that I had been exposed to Ulbarton's Flu a lot (the entire accounting department of the Pet Supply Catalogue Store, where I work, developed the flu. Also, my wife, three children, and mother-in-law. Plus, I believe my dog had it, though the vet disputes this.) However, despite all this exposure, I did not develop Ulbarton's.

My GP directed me to your research facility along I-270, saying he "thought he heard they were trying to develop a med." I went there, and samples of my blood and bodily tissues were taken. The researcher said I would hear from you if the samples were ever used for anything, but I never did. Will you please check your records to verify my participation in this new medicine and tell me what share of the profits are due me.

Thank you for your consideration.

Sincerely,
Jon Meese
Jonathan J. Meese

* * *

From the Desk of Robert Ballston
Kegelman-Ballston Corporation

To: Martin Blake, Legal
Re: Attached letter

Marty—
Is he a nut? Is this a problem?

Bob

* * *

INTERNAL MEMO
KEGELMAN-BALLSTON

To: Robert Ballston
From: Martin Blake

Re: Gene-line claimant Jonathan J. Meese

Bob—

I checked with Records over in Research and, yes, unfortunately this guy donated the tissue samples from which the gene line was developed that led to Halitex. Even more unfortunately, Meese's visit occurred just before we instituted the comprehensive waiver for all donors. However, I don't think Meese has any legal grounds here. Court precedents have upheld the corporate right to patent genes used in drug development. Also, the guy doesn't sound very sophisticated (his dog?). He doesn't even know that Kegelman's been dead for ten years. Apparently, Meese has not yet employed a lawyer. I can make a small nuisance settlement if you like, but I'd rather avoid setting a corporate precedent for these people. I'd rather send him a stiff letter that will scare the bejesus out of the greedy little twerp.

Please advise.

Marty

* * *

From the Desk of Robert Ballston
Kegelman-Ballston Corporation

To: Martin Blake, Legal

Re: J. Meese

Do it.

Bob

Martin Blake, Attorney-at-Law
Chief Legal Counsel, Kegelman-Ballston Corporation

Dear Mr. Meese,

Your letter regarding the patented Kegelman-Ballston drug Halitex has been referred to me. Please be advised that you have no legal rights in Halitex; see attached list of case precedents. If you persist in any such claims, Kegelman-Ballston will consider it harassment and take appropriate steps, including possible prosecution.

Sincerely,
Martin Blake
Martin Blake

* * *

Jonathan Meese
538 Pleasant Lane
Aspen Hill, MD 20906

Dear Mr. Blake,

But they're my genes!!! This can't be right. I'm consulting a lawyer, and you can expect to hear from her shortly.

Jon Meese
Jonathan J. Meese

Catherine Owen, Attorney-at-Law

Dear Mr. Blake,

I now represent Jonathan J. Meese in his concern that Kegelman-Ballston has developed a pharmaceutical, Halitex, based on gene therapy which uses Mr. Meese's genes as its basis. We feel it only reasonable that this drug, which will earn Kegelman-Ballston millions if not billions of dollars, acknowledge financially Mr. Meese's considerable contribution. We are therefore willing to consider a settlement and are available to discuss this with you at your earliest convenience.

Sincerely,

Catherine Owen
Catherine Owen, Attorney

* * *

From the Desk of Robert Ballston
Kegelman-Ballston Corporation

To: Martin Blake, Legal
Re: J. Meese

Marty—

Damn it, if there's one thing that really chews my balls it's this sort of undercover sabotage by the second-rate. I played golf with Sam Fortescue on Saturday and he opened my eyes (you remember Sam; he's at the agency we're using to benchmark our competition). Sam speculates that this Meese bastard is really being used by Irwin-Lacey to set us up. You know that bastard Carl Irwin has had his own Ulbarton's drug in development, and he's sore as hell because we beat him to market. Ten to one he's paying off this Meese patsy.

We can't allow it. Don't settle. Let him sue.

Bob

* * *

INTERNAL MEMO
KEGELMAN-BALLSTON

To: Robert Ballston
From: Martin Blake
Re: Gene-line claimant Jonathan J. Meese

Bob—

I've got a better idea. We sue him, on the grounds he's walking around with our patented genetic immunity to Ulbarton's. No one except consumers of Halitex have this immunity, so Meese must have acquired it illegally, possibly on the black market. We gain several advantages with this suit: We eliminate Meese's complaint; we send a clear message to other rivals who may be attempting patent infringement; we gain a publicity circus to both publicize Halitex (not that it needs it); and, more important, make the public aware of the dangers of black-market substitutes for Halitex, such as Meese obtained.

Incidentally, I checked again with Records over at Research. They have no documentation of any visit from a Jonathan J. Meese on any date whatsoever.

Marty

* * *

From the Desk of Robert Ballston
Kegelman-Ballston Corporation

To: Martin Blake, Legal
Re: J. Meese

Marty—

Brilliant! Do it. Can we get a sympathetic judge? One who understands business? Maybe O'Connor can help.

Bob

* * *

NEW YORK TIMES
HALITEX BLACK MARKET CASE TO BEGIN TODAY

This morning the circuit court of Manhattan County is scheduled to begin hearing the case of Kegelman-Ballston v. Meese. This case, heavily publicized during recent months, is expected to set important precedents in the controversial areas of gene patents and patent infringement on biological properties. Protestors from the group For Us: Cancel Kidnapped Ulbarton Patents, which is often referred to by its initials, have been in place on the court steps since last night. The case is being heard by Judge Latham P. Farmingham III, a Republican widely perceived as sympathetic to the concerns of big business.

This case began when Jonathan J. Meese, an accountant with the Pet Supply Catalogue Store . . .

* * *

Catherine Owen, Attorney-at-Law

Dear Mr. Blake,

Just a reminder that Jon Meese and I are still open to a settlement.

Sincerely,

Catherine Owen

* * *

Martin Blake, Attorney-at-Law
Chief Legal Counsel, Kegelman-Ballston Corporation

Cathy—

Don't they teach you at that law school you went to (I never can remember the name) that you don't settle when you're sure to win?

You're a nice girl; better luck next time.

Martin Blake

NEW YORK TIMES
MEESE CONVICTED

PLAINTIFF GUILTY OF "HARBORING" DISEASE-FIGHTING GENES WITHOUT COMPENSATING DEVELOPER KEGELMAN-BALLSTON

* * *

From the Desk of Robert Ballston
Kegelman-Ballston Corporation

To: Martin Blake, Legal
Re: Kegelman-Ballston v. Meese

Marty—

I always said you were a genius! My God, the free publicity we got out of this thing, not to mention the future edge . . . How about a victory celebration this weekend? Are you and Elaine free to fly to Aruba on the Lear, Friday night?

Bob

* * *

NEW YORK TIMES
BLUE GENES FOR DRUG THIEF

JONATHAN J. MEESE SENTENCED TO SIX MONTHS FOR PATENT INFRINGEMENT

* * *

From the Desk of Robert Ballston
Kegelman-Ballston Corporation

To: Martin Blake, Legal
Re: Halitex

Marty,

I just had a brilliant idea I want to run by you. We got Meese, but now that he's at Ossining, the publicity has died down. Well, my daughter read this squib the other day in some science magazine, how the Ulbarton's virus has in it some of the genes that Research combined with Meese's to create Halitex. I didn't understand all the egghead science, but apparently Halitex uses some of the flu genes to build its immune properties. And we own the patent on Halitex. As I see it, that means that Dr. Ulbarton was working with OUR genes when he identified Ulbarton's flu and published his work. Now, if we could go after Ulbarton in court, the publicity would be tremendous, as well as strengthening our proprietorship position.

But the publicity, Marty! The publicity!

Not What I Intended

Anyone who thinks that, at an early age, they can plan their entire life is mistaken. Anyone who thinks they can plan their child's entire life is delusional.

And yet that is what my mother and I, in cozy and staggeringly naïve collusion, did in 1960. I was twelve years old and still playing with Barbies, though not admitting this at school. That year, Texas Instruments patented the first integrated circuit silicon chip. The first laser was developed, the first birth-control pill was approved, the structure of hemoglobin determined, RNA polymerase discovered. I was unaware, and uninterested, in all of it. Three years earlier, Sputnik had flown through the night, igniting the space race. I was aware of that, but none of this seemed to have anything to do with my future.

My mother, the daughter of a Sicilian immigrant who could neither read or write in any language, was an utterly traditional 1950s wife and mother. She said to me, "Would you like to be a teacher, a nurse, or a secretary?" She could not conceive of any other occupation for a girl. I thought about it and said, "A teacher." I liked kids and was already babysitting my little sister.

"Good," she said. "If you're a teacher, you can have summers off to be with your own kids when you have them." For her, children were "when," not "if." She added, "Then you'll have to go to college."

So, I did, although not without a lot of negative comments from my great aunts in outspoken Italian. "Why are you sending Nancy to college? She's pretty enough to get a husband!" That was the thinking in that time and place in my huge extended family.

To her great credit, my mother persisted in the college plan. Neither of my parents had college degrees. I had always read all the fiction I could, asking for books as presents on every gift-giving occasion and then reciting the plots to my sister. (Much later she would resent me for it because every time she picked up a novel, she already knew the ending.) Books were my constant, my excitement, my solace. Yet it never crossed anyone's mind, including mine, that I might write, let alone write science fiction.

Especially science fiction, since I was fourteen before I saw any. We lived deep in the country and my mother could not drive, so trips to the local library were rare. The elementary school library was divided into a boys' section and a girls' section—the prefeminist 1950s were like that. At fourteen, I had my first boyfriend, a sixteen-year-old neighbor who was studying to be a concert pianist. After school, I would go to his house and hang adoringly over the piano while he practiced. Unfortunately, I am next-door to tone deaf, and ten minutes was all the adoration I could manage. His father had bookshelves in the room, and I began to pull out books and read. One of the first was Arthur C. Clarke's *Childhood's End*. Three pages in, and I was in love, and not with the pianist. Here was scope—an entire galaxy!—that I had not imagined. I began to read all the SF I could find. But not to dream of writing it; my future was already planned. Besides, writers were exalted, godlike beings who lived far away, whereas I was a girl in a homogenous, Wonder-bread-and-Jello-salad small town.

I was a freshman in college at a small state college, an elementary-education major, when *Star Trek* debuted. Immediately I was hooked. Not just "hooked"—obsessed. I saw the season's episodes, the summer reruns. I would stand—and this is embarrassing to admit now—in my father's back field, staring up at the stars and *willing* the *Enterprise* to be out there. Decades later, when the movie *Galaxy Quest* premiered, I knew exactly how Jason felt. My family thought I was insane.

After college, I taught the fourth grade for four years, married, had kids. The plan my mother and I had hatched for my life was holding—with an unexpected variation.

My then-husband and I had bought a house in the country. My thinking was that I had loved growing up in woods and fields and creek, so my kids would, too. I had not considered, and she did not tell me until much later, the isolation and frustration our house had imposed on my mother, a city girl whose idea of the outdoors was coffee on a patio. For our first year, the house my husband and I inhabited was on a road with few other houses, none of them occupied by women my age, or by anybody else since the older adults all went to work. My husband was taking an MBA in the city and had evening classes; frequently he just ate dinner downtown. I was alone nearly all the time with a toddler and a difficult pregnancy, followed by a second baby. I was going nuts.

When the babies napped, and out of sheer desperation for words of more than one syllable, I began to write. Out came speculative fiction. I had read a lot of science fiction, but I had read a lot of everything. Nonetheless, those initial stories were SF. Very bad SF. But I knew that you were supposed to put stories into manila envelopes and send them to the SF magazines, so I did that. The stories, initially terrible, must have improved, because after a year or so, one of them sold, "The Earth Dwellers." The only reason it did so, I later suspected, was that *Galaxy* was on the verge of folding and had stopped paying its writers, so writers had stopped submitting there. I knew nothing of that, nor of the professional association then called Science Fiction Writers of America (SFWA), conventions, fandom, or any of the other things that would eventually fill my professional life.

I had sold a story. Did that make me a writer? I didn't know. But I continued to write, and slowly to sell, although—and this seems incredible to me now—for the first few years, I did not take writing very seriously. It was not a career, but a sort of hobby. The serious things in my life were my kids, my marriage, my extended family, the graduate degree I was eking out one course at a time so that when my kids were old enough, I could return to teaching fourth grade.

At thirty-three, however, my life plan fell apart. It was amazing that it lasted that long. My marriage ended. There were no teaching jobs; it was the "baby bust" era when elementary schools were laying off teachers. I had sold a novel, *The Prince of Morning Bells*, and wanted to sell more. Writing had morphed into a central passion in my life, along with my two kids, and everything was restructured: new part-time job writing for an ad agency, supplemented by part-time teaching creative writing and freshman composition as adjunct faculty at the local state college. New friends at the SF cons I scraped together money to attend. I discovered that writers were not exalted, godlike beings after all. Eventually regular publication followed, then awards, and in 1990 I became a full-time writer.

None of this had been intended. Nor had the switch from writing fantasy to writing science fiction, and, as time went on, to writing hard science fiction, eagerly researching all that science I had never been much interested in during high school or college. Genetic engineering became almost as fascinating to me—*almost*—as fiction.

Why am I telling you in such detail about this personal odyssey? Let me broaden the perspective a little from the personal by stating some things my writing journey made clear to me.

First, it was a very female journey. Those of us who grew up in the 1950s, in working-class and/or immigrant families especially, experienced a far different world than boys of that era or girls born a few decades later, let alone the young women of today. We had, or at least some of us, internalized the limits we'd learned from our mothers and the larger culture. Eventually many of us pushed past those limits, some with the aid of second-wave feminism and, if we were lucky, with the encouragement of a few older people with wider perspectives on the world. Even so, the unfortunate and occasionally nasty split within feminism between those women with children and those who looked down on stay-at-home moms made the complicated struggle to raise kids while writing even more complicated. Would I have written earlier, or taking my writing more seriously earlier, had I been unmarried, or without children, or a male? There is no way to know. I do know, however, that few writers begin writing solely as an alternative to diapers and *Sesame Street*. Most I have talked to about their career paths say that they knew they wanted to be writers by their teenage years, or at twelve, ten, a few even younger.

Second, even among those who know early that they will be writers, there is amazing variation among career paths. A few SF writers I know had early, almost instant, success but that is certainly not the norm. Some decide young, then spend twenty years writing before a first publication. Some score a big sale or widely acclaimed book early on, then publish steadily but never hit that height again. Some go up, down, up, down like an unpredictable elevator. Some climb steadily, book by book. Some get a strong reputation as a short-story writer but can't write a good novel. Some are good novelists but can't write short stories. Some publish for a few years, stop writing to follow other pursuits, and years or decades later decide to resume writing.

Third, most successful writers are resourceful and determined because they have to be. Whining is allowed and pandemic, but it must not displace what is described by that useful German word *Sitzfleisch*, which basically means sit your butt down and do the work. If a person really wants to write, they will get up painfully early in the morning and write before the family is stirring. Or they will write late at night, fueled by coffee (or whatever). They will bargain with family and friends for uninterrupted time—"If you watch my kids for two hours this morning, I'll take yours tomorrow." They will curtail or give up golf, video games, chess, social media, long leisurely lunches, vacations, or whatever else can be traded for time to write. They will, if necessary, use every penny possible to buy more writing time, paying for babysitters or quiet office space. They don't blame not writing on their family backgrounds or their health or age or cultural zeitgeist or need to support a family. Writers have created fiction in gulags, prisons, bad marriages, bad jobs, war zones, overcrowded apartments without heat, hospital beds.

I knew none of this when I began writing. The writing life was not what I intended; I merely wanted a tiny relief from overwhelming domesticity. But intentions can change for many reasons, including that the intentions of the larger culture into which one was born may not match one's authentic identity. I stumbled into writing science fiction, but it turns out that is where I was meant to be all along.

Laws of Survival

My name is Jill. I am somewhere you can't imagine, going somewhere even more unimaginable. If you think I like what I did to get here, you're crazy.

Actually, I'm the one who's crazy. You—any "you"—will never read this. But I have paper now, and a sort of pencil, and time. Lots and lots of time. So, I will write what happened, all of it, as carefully as I can.

After all—why the hell not?

I went out very early one morning to look for food. Before dawn was safest for a woman alone. The boy-gangs had gone to bed, tired of attacking each other. The trucks from the city hadn't arrived yet. That meant the garbage was pretty picked over, but it also meant most of the refugee camp wasn't out scavenging. Most days I could find enough: a carrot stolen from somebody's garden patch, even if I had to bloody my arm from reaching through the barbed wire. Overlooked potato peelings under a pile of rags and glass. A half-full can of stew thrown away by one of the soldiers on the base. Soldiers on duty by the Dome were often careless. They got bored, with nothing to do.

That morning was cool but fair, with a pearly haze that the sun would burn off later. I wore all my clothing, for warmth, and my boots. Yesterday's garbage load, I'd heard somebody say, was huge, so I had hopes. I hiked to my favorite spot, where garbage spills almost to the Dome wall. Maybe I'd find bread, or even fruit that wasn't too rotten.

Instead, I found the puppy.

Its eyes weren't open yet and it squirmed along the bare ground, a scrawny brown-and-white mass with a tiny fluffy tail. Nearby was a fluid-soaked towel. Some sentimental fool had left the puppy there, hoping . . . what? It didn't matter. Scrawny or not, there was some meat on the thing. I scooped it up.

The sun pushed above the horizon, flooding the haze with golden light.

I hate it when grief seizes me. I hate it and it's dangerous, a violation of one of Jill's Laws of Survival. I can go for weeks, months without thinking of my life before the War. Without remembering or feeling. Then something will strike me—a flower growing in the dump, a burst of birdsong, the stars on a clear night—and grief will hit me like the maglevs that no longer exist, a grief all the sharper because it contains the memory of joy. I can't afford joy, which always comes with an astronomical price tag. I can't even afford the grief that comes from the memory of living things, which is why it is only the flower, the birdsong, the morning sunlight that starts it. My grief was not for that puppy. I still intended to eat it.

But I heard a noise behind me and turned. The Dome wall was opening.

Who knew why the aliens put their Domes by garbage dumps, by waste pits, by radioactive cities? Who knew why aliens did anything?

There was a widespread belief in the camp that the aliens had started the War. I'm old enough to know better. That was us, just like the global warming and the bio-crobes were us. The aliens didn't even show up until the War was over, Raleigh was the northernmost city left on the East Coast, and refugees started pouring south like mudslides. Including me. That's when the ships landed and then turned into the huge gray Domes like upended bowls. I heard there were many Domes, some in other countries. The Army, what was left of it, threw tanks and bombs at ours. When they gave up, the refugees threw bullets and Molotov cocktails and prayers and graffiti and candlelight vigils and rain dances. Everything slid off and the Domes just sat there. And sat. And sat. Three years later, they were still sitting, silent and closed, although of course there were rumors to the contrary. There are always rumors. Personally, I'd never gotten over a slight disbelief that the Dome was there at all. Who would want to visit us?

The opening was small, no larger than a porthole, and about six feet above the ground. All I could see inside was a fog the same color as the Dome. Something came out, gliding quickly toward me. It took me a moment to realize it was a robot, a blue metal sphere above a hanging basket. It stopped a foot from my face and said, "This food, in exchange for that dog."

I could have run, or screamed, or at the least—the very least—looked around for a witness. I didn't. The basket held a pile of fresh produce, green lettuce and deep purple eggplant and apples so shiny red they looked lacquered. And *peaches* . . . My mouth filled with sweet water. I couldn't move.

The puppy whimpered.

My mother used to make fresh peach pie.

I scooped the food into my scavenger bag, laid the puppy in the basket, and backed away. The robot floated back into the Dome, which closed immediately. I sped back to my corrugated-tin and windowless hut and ate until I couldn't hold any more. I slept, woke, and ate the rest, crouching in the dark so nobody else would see. All that fruit and vegetables gave me the runs, but it was worth it.

Peaches.

Two weeks later, I brought another puppy to the Dome, the only survivor of a litter deep in the dump. I never knew what happened to the mother. I had to wait a long time outside the Dome before the blue sphere took the puppy in exchange for produce. Apparently, the Dome would only open when there was no one else around to see. What were they afraid of? It's not like PETA was going to show up.

The next day I traded three of the peaches to an old man in exchange for a small, mangy poodle. We didn't look each other in the eye, but I nonetheless knew that his held tears. He limped hurriedly away. I kept the dog, which clearly wanted nothing to do with me, in my shack until very early morning and then took it to the Dome. It tried to escape but I'd tied a bit of rope onto its frayed collar. We sat outside the Dome in mutual dislike, waiting, as the sky paled slightly in the east. Gunshots sounded in the distance.

I have never owned a dog.

When the Dome finally opened, I gripped the dog's rope and spoke to the robot. "Not fruit. Not vegetables. I want eggs and bread."

The robot floated back inside.

Instantly I cursed myself. Eggs? Bread? I was crazy not to take what I could get. That was Law of Survival #1. Now there would be nothing. Eggs, bread . . . *crazy*. I glared at the dog and kicked it. It yelped, looked indignant, and tried to bite my boot.

The Dome opened again and the robot glided toward me. In the gloom I couldn't see what was in the basket. In fact, I couldn't see the basket. It wasn't there. Mechanical tentacles shot out from the sphere and seized both me and the poodle. I cried out and the tentacles squeezed harder. Then I was flying through the air, the stupid dog suddenly howling beneath me, and we were carried through the Dome wall and inside.

Then nothing.

A nightmare room made of nightmare sound: barking, yelping, whimpering, snapping. I jerked awake, sat up, and discovered myself on a floating platform above a mass of dogs. Big dogs, small dogs, old dogs, puppies, sick dogs, dogs that looked all too healthy, flashing their forty-two teeth at me—why did I remember that number? From where? The largest and strongest dogs couldn't quite reach me with their snaps, but they were trying.

"You are operative," the blue metal sphere said, floating beside me. "Now we must begin. Here."

Its basket held eggs and bread.

"Get them away!"

Obediently it floated off.

"Not the food! The dogs!"

"What to do with these dogs?"

"Put them in cages!" A large black animal—German Shepherd or Boxer or something—had nearly closed its jaws on my ankle. The next bite might do it.

"Cages," the metal sphere said in its uninflected mechanical voice. "Yes."

"Son of a bitch!" The Shepherd, leaping high, gazed my thigh; its spittle slimed my pants. "Raise the goddamn platform!"

"Yes."

The platform floated so high, so that I had to duck my head to avoid hitting the ceiling. I peered over the edge and . . . no, that wasn't possible. But it was happening. The floor was growing upright sticks, and the sticks were growing cross bars, and the crossbars were extending themselves into mesh tops . . . Within minutes, each dog was encased in a cage just large enough to hold its protesting body.

"What to do now?" the metal sphere asked.

I stared at it. I was, as far as I knew, the first human being to ever enter an alien Dome, I was trapped in a small room with feral caged dogs and a robot . . . *what to do now*?

"Why . . . why am I here?" I hated myself for the brief stammer and vowed it would not happen again. Law of Survival #2: Show no fear.

Would a metal sphere even recognize fear?

It said, "These dogs do not behave correctly."

"Not behave correctly?"

"No."

I looked down again at the slavering and snarling mass of dogs; how strong was that mesh on the cage tops? "What do you want them to do?"

"You want to see the presentation?"

"Not yet." Law #3: Never volunteer for anything.

"What to do now?"

How the hell should I know? But the smell of the bread reached me and my stomach flopped. "Now to eat," I said. "Give me the things in your basket."

It did, and I tore into the bread like a wolf into deer. The real wolves below me increased their howling. When I'd eaten an entire loaf, I looked back at the metal sphere. "Have those dogs eaten?"

"Yes."

"What did you give them?"

"Garbage."

"*Garbage*? Why?"

"In hell they eat garbage."

So even the robot thought this was Hell. Panic surged through me; I pushed it back. Surviving this would depend on staying steady. "Show me what you fed the dogs."

"Yes." A section of wall melted and garbage cascaded into the room, flowing greasily between the cages. I recognized it: It was exactly like the garbage I picked through every day, trucked out from a city I could no longer imagine and from the Army base I could not approach without being shot. Bloody rags, tin cans from before the War, shit, plastic bags, dead flowers, dead animals, dead electronics, cardboard, eggshells, paper, hair, bone, scraps of decaying food, glass shards, potato peelings, foam rubber, roaches, sneakers with holes, sagging furniture, corn cobs. The smell hit my stomach, newly distended with bread.

"You fed the dogs *that*?"

"Yes. They eat it in hell."

Outside. Hell was outside, and of course that's what the feral dogs ate, that's all there was. But the metal sphere had produced fruit and lettuce and bread for me.

"You must give them better food. They eat that in . . . in hell because they can't get anything else."

"What to do now?"

It finally dawned on me—slow, I was too slow for this, only the quick survive—that the metal sphere had limited initiative along with its limited vocabulary. But it had made cages, made bread, made fruit—hadn't it? Or was this stuff grown in some imaginable secret garden inside the Dome? "You must give the dogs meat."

"Flesh?"

"Yes."

"No."

No change in that mechanical voice, but the "no" was definite and quick. Law of Survival #4: Notice everything. So—no flesh-eating allowed here. Also no time to ask why not; I had to keep issuing orders so that the robot didn't start issuing them. "Give them bread mixed with . . . with soy protein."

"Yes."

"And take away the garbage."

"Yes."

The garbage began to dissolve. I saw nothing poured on it, nothing rise from the floor. But all that stinking mass fell into powder and vanished. Nothing replaced it.

I said, "Are you getting bread mixed with soy powder?" *Getting* seemed the safest verb I could think of.

"Yes."

The stuff came then, tumbling through the same melted hole in the wall, loaves of bread with, presumably, soy powder in them. The dogs, barking insanely, reached paws and snouts and tongues through the bars of their cages. They couldn't get at the food.

"Metal sphere—do you have a name?"

No answer.

"Okay. Blue, how strong are those cages? Can the dogs break them? Any of the dogs?"

"No."

"Lower the platform to the floor."

My safe perch floated down. The aisles between the cages were irregular, some wide and some so narrow the dogs could reach through to touch each other, since each cage had "grown" wherever the dog was at the time. Gingerly I picked my way to a clearing and sat down. Tearing a loaf of bread into chunks, I pushed the pieces through the bars of the least dangerous-looking dogs, which made the bruisers howl even more. For them, I put chunks at a distance they could just reach with a paw through the front bars of their prisons.

The puppy I had first brought to the Dome lay in a tiny cage. Dead.

The second one was alive but just barely.

The old man's mangy poodle looked mangier than ever, but otherwise alert. It tried to bite me when I fed it.

"What to do now?"

"They need water."

"Yes."

Water flowed through the wall. When it had reached an inch or so, it stopped. The dogs lapped whatever came into their cages. I stood with wet feet—a hole in my boot after all, I hadn't known—and a stomach roiling from the stench of the dogs, which only worsened as they got wet. The dead puppy smelled especially horrible. I climbed back onto my platform.

"What to do now?"

"You tell me," I said.

"These dogs do not behave correctly."

"Not behave correctly?"

"No."

"What do you want them to do?"

"Do you want to see the presentation?"

We had been here before. On second thought, a "presentation" sounded more like acquiring information ("Notice everything") than like undertaking action ("Never volunteer"). So, I sat cross-legged on the platform, which was easier on my uncushioned bones, breathed through my mouth instead of my nose, and said "Why the hell not?"

Blue repeated, "Do you want to see the presentation?"

"Yes." A one-syllable answer.

I didn't know what to expect. Aliens, spaceships, war, strange places barely comprehensible to humans. What I got was scenes from the dump.

A beam of light shot out from Blue and resolved into a three-dimensional holo, not too different from one I'd seen in a science museum on a school field trip once (*no. push memory away*), only this was far sharper and detailed. A ragged and unsmiling toddler, one of thousands, staggered toward a cesspool. A big dog with patchy coat dashed up, seized the kid's dress, and pulled her back just before she fell into the waste.

A medium-sized brown dog in a guide-dog harness led around someone tapping a white-headed cane.

An Army dog, this one sleek and well-fed, sniffed at a pile of garbage, found something, pointed stiffly at attention.

A group of teenagers tortured a puppy. It writhed in pain, but in a long lingering close-up, tried to lick the torturer's hand,

A thin, small dog dodged rocks, dashed inside a corrugated tin hut, and laid a piece of carrion beside an old lady lying on the ground.

The holo went on and on like that, but the strange thing was that the people were barely seen. The toddler's bare and filthy feet and chubby knees, the old lady's withered cheek, a flash of a camouflage uniform above a brown boot, the hands of the torturers. Never a whole person, never a focus on people. Just on the dogs.

The "presentation" ended.

"These dogs do not behave correctly," Blue said.

"These dogs? In the presentation?"

"These dogs here do not behave correctly."

"These dogs *here*." I pointed to the wet, stinking dogs in their cages. Some, fed now, had quieted. Others still snarled and barked, trying their hellish best to get out and kill me.

"These dogs here. Yes. What to do now?"

"You want these dogs to behave like the dogs in the presentation."

"These dogs here must behave correctly. Yes."

"You want them to . . . do what? Rescue people? Sniff out

ammunition dumps? Guide the blind and feed the hungry and love their torturers?"

Blue said nothing. Again I had the impression I had exceeded its thought processes, or its vocabulary, or its something. A strange feeling gathered in my gut.

"Blue, you yourself didn't build this Dome, or the starship that it was before, did you? You're just a . . . a computer."

Nothing.

"Blue, who tells you what to do?"

"What to do now? These dogs do not behave correctly."

"Who wants these dogs to behave correctly?" I said, and found I was holding my breath.

"The masters."

The masters. I knew all about them. Masters were the people who started wars, ran the corporations that ruined the Earth, manufactured the bioweapons that killed billions, and now holed up in the cities to send their garbage out to us in the refugee camps. Masters were something else I didn't think about, but not because grief would take me. Rage would.

Law of Survival #5: Feel nothing that doesn't aid survival.

"Are the masters here? In this . . . inside here?"

"No."

"Who is here inside?"

"These dogs here are inside."

Clearly. "The masters want these dogs here to behave like the dogs in the presentation."

"Yes."

"The masters want these dogs here to provide them with loyalty and protection and service."

No response.

"The masters aren't interested in human beings, are they? That's why they haven't communicated at all with any government."

Nothing. But I didn't need a response; the masters' thinking was already clear to me. Humans were unimportant—maybe because we had, after all, destroyed each other and our own world. We weren't worth contact. But dogs: companion animals capable of selfless service and great unconditional love, even in the face of abuse. For all I knew, dogs were unique in the universe. For all I know.

Blue said, "What to do now?"

I stared at the mangy, reeking, howling mass of animals. Some feral, some tamed once, some sick, at least one dead. I chose my words to be as simple as possible, relying on phrases Blue knew. "The masters want these dogs here to behave correctly."

"Yes."

"The masters want *me* to make these dogs behave correctly."

"Yes."

"The masters will make me food, and keep me inside, for to make these dogs behave correctly."

Long pause; my sentence had a lot of grammatical elements. But finally Blue said, "Yes."

"If these dogs do not behave correctly, the masters—what to do then?"

Another long pause. "Find another human."

"And *this* human here?"

"Kill it."

I gripped the edges of my floating platform hard. My hands still trembled. "Put me outside now."

"No."

"I must stay inside."

"These dogs do not behave correctly."

"I must make these dogs behave correctly."

"Yes."

"And the masters want these dogs to display . . ." I had stopped talking to Blue. I was talking to myself, to steady myself, but even that I couldn't manage. The words caromed around in my mind—loyalty, service, protection—but none came out of my mouth. I couldn't do this. I was going to die. The aliens had come from God-knew-where to treat the dying Earth like a giant pet store, intrigued only by a canine domestication that had happened ten thousand years ago and by nothing else on the planet, nothing else humanity had or might accomplish. Only dogs. *The masters want these dogs to display—*

Blue surprised me with a new word. "Love," it said.

* * *

Law #4: Notice everything. I needed to learn all I could, starting with Blue. He'd made garbage appear, and food and water and cages. What else could he do?

"Blue, make the water go away." And it did, just sank into the floor, which dried instantly. I was fucking Moses, commanding the Red Sea. I climbed off the platform, inched among the dog cages, and studied them individually.

"You called the refugee camp and the dump 'hell.' Where did you get that word?"

Nothing.

"Who said 'hell'?"

"Humans."

Blue had cameras outside the Dome. Of course he did; he'd seen me find that first puppy in the garbage. Maybe Blue had been waiting for someone like me, alone and nonthreatening, to come close with a dog. But it had watched before that, and it had learned the word "hell," and maybe it had recorded the incidents in the "presentation." I filed this information for future use.

"This dog is dead." The first puppy, decaying into stinking pulp. "It is killed. Nonoperative."

"What to do now?"

"Make the dead dog go away."

A long pause: thinking it over? Accessing data banks? Communicating with aliens? And what kind of moron couldn't figure out by itself that a dead dog was never going to behave correctly? So much for artificial intelligence.

"Yes," Blue finally said, and the little corpse dissolved as if it had never been.

I found one more dead dog and one close to death. Blue disappeared the first, said no to the second. Apparently, we had to just let it suffer until it died. I wondered how much the idea of "death" even meant to a robot. There were twenty-three live dogs, of which I had delivered only three to the Dome.

"Blue—did another human, before you brought me here, try to train the dogs?"

"These dogs do not behave correctly."

"Yes. But did a human *not me* be inside? To make these dogs behave correctly?"

"Yes."

"What happened to him or her?"

No response.

"What to do now with the other human?"

"Kill it."

I put a hand against the wall and leaned on it. The wall felt smooth and slick, with a faint and unpleasant tingle. I removed my hand.

All computers could count. "How many humans did you kill?"

"Two."

Three's the charm. But there were no charms. No spells, no magic wards, no cavalry coming over the hill to ride to the rescue; I'd known that ever since the War. There was just survival. And, now, dogs.

I chose the mangy little poodle. It hadn't bitten me when the old man had surrendered it, or when I'd kept it overnight. That was at least a start. "Blue, make this dog's cage go away. But *only* this one cage!"

The cage dissolved. The poodle stared at me distrustfully. Was I supposed to stare back, or would that get us into some kind of canine pissing contest? The thing was small but it had teeth.

I had a sudden idea. "Blue, show me how this dog does not behave correctly." If I could see what it wasn't doing, that would at least be a start.

Blue floated to within a foot of the dog's face. The dog growled and backed away. Blue floated away and the dog quieted but it still stood in what would be a menacing stance if it weighed more than nine or ten pounds: ears raised, legs braced, neck hair bristling. Blue said, "Come." The dog did nothing. Blue repeated the entire sequence and so did Mangy.

I said, "You want the dog to follow you. Like the dogs in the presentation."

"Yes."

"You want the dog to come when you say 'Come,'"

"Love," Blue said.

"What is 'love,' Blue?"

No response.

The robot didn't know. Its masters must have had some concept of "love," but fuck-all knew what it was. And I wasn't sure I knew any more, either. That left Mangy, who would never "love" Blue or follow him or lick his hand because dogs operated on smell—even I knew that about them—and Blue, a machine, didn't smell like either a person or another dog. Couldn't the aliens who sent him here figure that out? Were they watching this whole farce, or had they just dropped a half-sentient computer under an upturned bowl on Earth and told it, "Bring us some loving dogs"? Who knew how aliens thought?

I didn't even know how dogs thought. There were much better people for this job—professional trainers, or that guy on TV who made tigers jump through burning hoops. But they weren't here, and I was. I squatted on my haunches a respectful distance from Mangy and said, "Come."

It growled at me.

"Blue, raise the platform this high." I held my hand at shoulder height. The platform rose.

"Now make some cookies on the platform."

Nothing.

"Make some . . . cheese on the platform."

Nothing. You don't see much cheese in a dump.

"Make some bread on the platform."

Nothing. Maybe the platform wasn't user-friendly.

"Make some bread."

After a moment, loaves tumbled out of the wall. "Enough! Stop!"

Mangy had rushed over to the bread, tearing at it, and the other dogs were going wild. I picked up one loaf, put it on the platform, and said, "Make the rest of the bread go away."

It all dissolved. No wonder the dogs were wary; I felt a little dizzy myself. A sentence from so long-ago child's book rose in my mind: *Things come and go so quickly here!*

I had no idea how much Blue could, or would, do on my orders. "Blue, make another room for me and this one dog. Away from the other dogs."

"No."

"Make this room bigger."

The room expanded evenly on all sides. "Stop." It did. "Make only this end of the room bigger."

Nothing.

"Okay, make the whole room bigger."

When the room stopped expanding, I had a space about forty feet square, with the dog cages huddled in the middle. After half an hour of experimenting, I got the platform moved to one corner, not far enough to escape the dog stench but better than nothing. (Law #1: Take what you can get.) I got a depression in the floor filled with warm water. I got food, drinking water, soap, and some clean cloth, and a lot of rope. By distracting Mangy with bits of bread, I got rope onto her frayed collar. After I got into the warm water and scrubbed myself, I pulled the poodle in. She bit me. But somehow I got her washed, too. Afterwards she shook herself, glared at me, and went to sleep on the hard floor. I asked Blue for a soft rug.

He said, "The other humans did this."

And Blue killed them anyway.

"Shut up," I said.

The big windowless room had no day, no night, no sanity. I slept and ate when I needed to, and otherwise I worked. Blue never left. He was an oversized, all-seeing eye in the corner. Big Brother, or God.

Within a few weeks—maybe—I had Mangy trained to come when called, to sit, and to follow me on command. I did this by dispensing bits of bread and other goodies. Mangy got fatter. I didn't care if she ended up the Fat Fiona of dogs. Her mange didn't improve, since I couldn't get Blue to wrap his digital mind around the concept of medicines, and even if he had I wouldn't have known what to ask for. The sick puppy died in its cage.

I kept the others fed and watered and flooded the shit out of their cages every day, but that was all. Mangy took all my time. She still regarded me warily, never curled up next to me, and occasionally growled. Love was not happening here.

Nonetheless, Blue left his corner and spoke for the first time in a week, scaring the hell out of me. "This dog behaves correctly."

"Well, thanks. I tried to . . . no, Blue . . . "

Blue floated to within a foot of Mangy's face, said, "Follow," and floated away. Mangy sat down and began to lick one paw. Blue rose and floated toward me.

"This dog does not behave correctly."

I was going to die.

"No, listen to me—listen! The dog can't smell you! It behaves for humans because of humans' smell! Do you understand?"

"No. This dog does not behave correctly."

"Listen! How the hell can you learn anything if you don't listen? You have to have a smell! Then the dog will follow you!"

Blue stopped. We stood frozen, a bizarre tableau, while the robot considered. Even Mangy stopped licking her paw and watched, still. They say dogs can smell fear.

Finally Blue said, "What is smell?"

It isn't possible to explain smell. Can't be done. Instead I pulled down my pants, tore the cloth I was using as underwear from between my legs, and rubbed it all over Blue, who did not react. I hoped he wasn't made of the same stuff as the Dome, which even spray paint had just slid off of. But, of course, he was. So I tied the strip of cloth around him with a piece of rope, my fingers trembling. "Now try the dog, Blue."

"Follow," Blue said, and floated away from Mangy.

She looked at him, then at me, then back at the floating metal sphere. I held my breath from some insane idea that I would thereby diminish my own smell. Mangy didn't move.

"This dog does not be—"

"She will if I'm gone!" I said desperately. "She smells me *and* you . . . and we smell the same so it's confusing her! But she'll follow you fine if I'm gone. Do you understand?"

"No."

"Blue . . . I'm going to get on the platform. See, I'm doing it. Raise the platform *very high*, Blue. Very high."

A moment later my head and ass both pushed against the ceiling, squishing me. I couldn't see what was happening below. I heard Blue say, "Follow," and I squeezed my eyes shut, waiting. My life depended on a scrofulous poodle with a gloomy disposition.

Blue said, "This dog behaves correctly."

He lowered my platform to a few yards above the floor, and I swear that—eyeless as he is and with part of his sphere obscured by my underwear—he looked right at me.

"This dog does behave correctly. This dog is ready."

"Ready? For . . . for what?"

Blue didn't answer. The next minute the floor opened and Mangy, yelping, tumbled into it. The floor closed. At the same time, one of the cages across the room dissolved and a German Shepherd hurtled toward me. I shrieked and yelled, "Raise the platform!" It rose just before the monster grabbed me.

Blue said, "What to do now? This dog does not behave correctly."

"For God's sakes, Blue—"

"This dog must love."

The shepherd leapt and snarled, teeth bared.

* * *

I couldn't talk Blue out of the Shepherd, which was as feral and vicious and unrelenting as anything in a horror movie. Or as Blue himself, in his own mechanical way. So, I followed the First Law: Take what you can get.

"Blue, make garbage again. A lot of garbage, right here." I pointed to the wall beside my platform.

"No."

Garbage, like everything else, apparently was made—or released, or whatever—from the opposite wall. I resigned myself to this. "Make a lot of garbage, Blue."

Mountains of stinking debris cascaded from the wall, spilling over until it reached the dog cages.

"Now stop. Move my platform above the garbage."

The platform moved. The caged dogs howled. Uncaged, the Shepherd poked eagerly in the refuse, too distracted to pay much attention to me. I had Blue lower the platform and I poked among it, too, keeping one eye on Vicious. If Blue was creating the garbage and not just trucking it in, he was doing a damn fine job of duplication. Xerox should have made such good copies.

I got smeared with shit and rot, but I found what I was looking for. The box was nearly a quarter full. I stuffed bread into it, coated the bread thoroughly, and discarded the box back onto the pile.

"Blue, make the garbage go away."

It did. Vicious glared at me and snarled. "Nice doggie," I said, "have some bread." I threw pieces and Vicious gobbled them.

Listening to the results was terrible. Not, however, as terrible as having Vicious tear me apart or Blue vaporize me. The rat poison took all "night" to kill the dog, which thrashed and howled. Throughout, Blue stayed silent. He had picked up some words from me, but he apparently didn't have enough brain power to connect what I'd done with Vicious's death. Or maybe he just didn't have enough experience with humans. What does a machine know about survival?

"This dog is dead," Blue said in the "morning."

"Yes. Make it go away." And then, before Blue could get there first, I jumped off my platform and pointed to a cage. "This dog will behave correctly next."

"No."

"Why not this dog?"

"Not big."

"Big. You want big." Frantically I scanned the cages, before Blue could choose another one like Vicious. "This one, then."

"Why the hell not?" Blue said.

It was young. Not a puppy but still frisky, a mongrel of some sort with short hair of dirty white speckled with dirty brown. The dog looked like something I could handle: big but not too big, not too aggressive, not too old, not too male. "Hey, Not-Too," I said, without enthusiasm, as Blue dissolved her cage. The mutt dashed over to me and tried to lick my boot.

A natural-born slave.

I had found a piece of rotten, moldy cheese in the garbage, so Blue could now make cheese, which Not-Too went crazy for. Not-Too and I stuck with the same routine I used with Mangy, and it worked pretty well. Or the cheese did. Within a few "days" the dog could sit, stay, and follow on command.

Then Blue threw me a curve. "What to do now? The presentation."

"We had the presentation," I said. "I don't need to see it again."

"What to do now? The presentation."

"Fine," I said, because it was clear I had no choice. "Let's have the presentation. Roll 'em."

I was sitting on my elevated platform, combing my hair. A lot of it had fallen out during the malnourished years in the camp, but now it was growing again. Not-Too had given up trying to jump up there with me and gone to sleep on her pillow below. Blue shot the beam out of his sphere and the holo played in front of me.

Only not the whole thing. This time he played only the brief scene where the big, patchy dog pulled the toddler back from falling into the cesspool. Blue played it once, twice, three times. Cold slid along my spine.

"You want Not-Too . . . you want this dog here to be trained to save children."

"This dog here does not behave correctly."

"Blue . . . How can I train a dog to save a child?"

"This dog here does not behave correctly."

"Maybe you haven't noticed, but we haven't got any fucking children for the dog to practice on!"

Long pause. "Do you want a child?"

"No!" Christ, he would kidnap one or buy one from the camp and I would be responsible for a kid along with nineteen semiferal dogs. No.

"This dog here does not behave correctly. What to do now? The presentation."

"No, not the presentation. I saw it, *I saw it.* Blue . . . the other two humans who did not make the dogs behave correctly . . ."

"Killed."

"Yes. So, you said. But they did get one dog to behave correctly, didn't they? Or maybe more than one. And then you just kept raising the bar higher. Water rescues, guiding the blind, finding lost people. Higher and higher."

But to all this, of course, Blue made no answer.

I racked my brains to remember what I had ever heard, read, or seen about dog training. Not much. However, there's a problem with opening the door to memory: you can't control what strolls through. For the first time in years, my sleep was shattered by dreams.

I walked through a tiny garden, picking zinnias. From an open window came music, full and strong, an orchestra on CD. A cat paced beside me, purring. And there was someone else in the window, someone who called my name and I turned and—

I screamed. Clawed my way upright. The dogs started barking and howling. Blue floated from his corner, saying something. And Not-Too made a mighty leap, landed on my platform, and began licking my face.

"Stop it! Don't do that! I won't remember!" I shoved her so hard she fell off the platform onto the floor and began yelping. I put my head in my hands.

Blue said, "Are you not operative?"

"Leave me the fuck alone!"

Not-Too still yelped, shrill cries of pain. When I stopped shaking, I crawled off the platform and picked her up. Nothing seemed to be broken—although how would I know? Gradually she quieted. I gave her some cheese and put her back on her pillow. She wanted to stay with me but I wouldn't let her.

I would not remember. *I would not.* Law #5: Feel nothing.

We made a cesspool, or at least a pool. Blue depressed part of the floor to a depth of three feet and filled it with water. Not-Too considered this a swimming pool and loved to be in it, which was not what Blue wanted ("This water does not behave correctly"). I tried having the robot dump various substances into it until I found one that she disliked and I could tolerate: light-grade motor oil. A few small cans of oil like those in the dump created a polluted pool, not unlike Charleston Harbor. After every practice session I needed a bath.

But not Not-Too, because she wouldn't go into the "cesspool." I curled myself as small as possible, crouched at the side of the pool, and thrashed. After a few days, the dog would pull me back by my shirt. I moved into the pool. As long as she could reach me without getting any liquid on her, Not-Too happily played that game. As soon as I moved far enough out that I might actually need saving, she sat on her skinny haunches and looked away.

"This dog does not behave correctly."

I increased the cheese. I withheld the cheese. I pleaded and ordered and shunned and petted and yelled. Nothing worked. Meanwhile, the dream continued. The same dream, each time not greater in length but increasing in intensity. *I walked through a tiny garden, picking zinnias. From an open window came music, full and strong, an orchestra on CD. A cat paced beside me, purring. And there was someone else in the window, someone who called my name and I turned and—*

And woke screaming.

A cat. I had had a cat, before the War. Before everything. I had always had cats, my whole life. Independent cats, aloof and self-sufficient, admirably disdainful. Cats—

The dog below me whimpered, trying to get onto my platform to offer comfort I did not want.

I would not remember.

"This dog does not behave correctly," day after day.

I had Blue remove the oil from the pool. But by now Not-Too had been conditioned. She wouldn't go into even the clear water that she'd reveled in before.

"This dog does not behave correctly."

Then one day Blue stopped his annoying mantra, which scared me even more. Would I have any warning that I'd failed, or would I just die?

The only thing I could think of was to kill Blue first.

* * *

Blue was a computer. You disabled computers by turning them off, or cutting the power supply, or melting them in a fire, or dumping acid on them, or crushing them. But a careful search of the whole room revealed no switches or wires or anything that looked like a wireless control. A fire in this closed room, assuming

I could start one, would kill me, too. Every kind of liquid or solid slid off Blue. And what would I crush him with, if that was even possible? A piece of cheese?

Blue was also—sort of—an intelligence. You could kill those by trapping them somewhere. My prison-or-sanctuary (depending on my mood) had no real "somewheres." And Blue would just dissolve any structure he found himself in.

What to do now?

I lay awake, thinking, all night, which at least kept me from dreaming, I came up with two ideas, both bad. Plan A depended on discussion, never Blue's strong suit.

"Blue, this dog does not behave correctly."

"No."

"This dog is not operative. I must make another dog behave correctly. Not this dog."

Blue floated close to Not-Too. She tried to bat at him. He circled her slowly, then returned to his position three feet above the ground. "This dog is operative."

"No. This dog *looks* operative. But this dog is not operative inside its head. I cannot make this dog behave correctly. I need a different dog."

A very long pause. "This dog is not operative inside its head."

"*Yes.*"

"You can make another dog behave correctly. Like the presentation."

"Yes." It would at least buy me time. Blue must have seen "not operative" dogs and humans in the dump; God knows there were enough of them out there. Madmen, rabid animals, druggies raving just before they died, or were shot. And next time I would add something besides oil to the pool; there must be something that Blue would consider noxious enough to simulate a cesspool but that a dog would enter. If I had to, I'd use my own shit.

"This dog is not operative inside its head," Blue repeated, getting used to the idea. "You will make a different dog behave correctly."

"Yes!"

"Why the hell not?" And then, "I kill this dog."

"No!" The word was torn from me before I knew I was going to say anything. My hand, of its own volition, clutched at Not-Too. She jumped but didn't bite. Instead, maybe sensing my fear, she cowered behind me, and I started to yell.

"You can't just kill everything that doesn't behave like you want! People, dogs . . . you can't just kill everything! You can't just . . . I had a cat . . . I never wanted a dog but this dog . . . she's behaving correctly for her! For a fucking traumatized dog and you can't just—I had a dog I mean a cat I had . . . I had. . . "

—from an open window came music, full and strong, an orchestra on CD. A cat paced beside me, purring. And there was someone else in the window, someone who called my name and I turned and—

"I had a child!"

Oh, God no no no . . . It all came out then, the memories and the grief and the pain I had pushed away for three solid years in order to survive . . . *Feel nothing* . . . Zack Zack *Zack* shot down by soldiers like a dog *Look, Mommy, here I am Mommy look* . . .

I curled in a ball on the floor and screamed and wanted to die. Grief had been postponed so long that it was a tsunami. I sobbed and screamed; I don't know for how long. I think I wasn't quite sane. No human should ever have to experience that much pain. But of course they do.

However, it can't last too long, that height of pain, and when the flood passed and my head was bruised from banging it on the hard floor, I was still alive, still inside the Dome, still surrounded by barking dogs. Zack was still dead. Blue floated nearby, unchanged, a casually murderous robot who would not supply flesh to dogs as food but who would kill anything he was programmed to destroy. And he had no reason not to murder me.

Not-Too sat on her haunches, regarding me from sad brown eyes, and I did the one thing I told myself I never would do again. I reached for her warmth. I put my arms around her and hung on. She let me.

Maybe that was the decision point. I don't know.

When I could manage it, I staggered to my feet. Taking hold of the rope that was Not-Too's leash, I wrapped it firmly around my hand. "Blue," I said, forcing the words past the grief clogging my throat, "make garbage."

He did. The basis of Plan B was that Blue made most things I asked of him. Not release, or mercy, but at least rooms and platforms and pools and garbage. I walked toward the garbage spilling from the usual place in the wall.

"More garbage! Bigger garbage! I need garbage to make this dog behave correctly!"

The reeking flow increased. Tires, appliances, diapers, rags, cans, furniture. The dogs' howling rose to an insane, deafening pitch. Not-Too pressed close to me.

"Bigger garbage!"

The chassis of a motorcycle, twisted beyond repair in some unimaginable accident, crashed into the room. The place on the wall from which the garbage spewed was misty gray, the same fog that the Dome had become when I had been taken inside it. Half a sofa clattered through. I grabbed Not-Too, dodged behind the sofa, and hurled both of us through the onrushing garbage and into the wall.

A broken keyboard struck me in the head, and the gray went black.

Chill. Cold with a spot of heat, which turned out to be Not-Too lying on top of me. I pushed her off and tried to sit up. Pain lanced through my head and when I put a hand to my forehead, it came away covered with blood. The same blood streamed into my eyes, making it hard to see. I wiped the blood away with the front of my shirt, pressed my hand hard on my forehead, and looked around.

Not that there was much to see. The dog and I sat at the end of what appeared to be a corridor. Above me loomed a large machine of some type, with a chute pointed at the now-solid wall. The machine was silent. Not-Too quivered and pressed her furry side into mine, but she, too, stayed silent. I couldn't hear the nineteen dogs on the other side of the wall, couldn't see Blue, couldn't smell anything except Not-Too, who had made a small yellow puddle on the floor.

There was no room to stand upright under the machine, so I moved away from it. Strips ripped from the bottom of my shirt made a bandage that at least kept blood out of my eyes. Slowly Not-Too and I walked along the corridor.

No doors. No openings or alcoves or machinery. Nothing until we reached the end, which was the same uniform material as everything else. Gray, glossy, hard. Dead.

Blue did not appear. Nothing appeared, or disappeared, or lived. We walked back and studied the overhead bulk of the machine. It had no dials or keys or features of any kind.

I sat on the floor, largely because I couldn't think what else to do, and Not-Too climbed into my lap. She was too big for this, and I pushed her away. She pressed against me, trembling.

"Hey," I said, but not to her. Zack in the window *Look, Mommy, here I am Mommy look . . .* But if I started down that mental road, I would be lost. Anger was better than memory. Anything was better than memory. "Hey!" I screamed. "Hey, you bastard Blue, what to do now? What to do now, you Dome shits, whoever you are?"

Nothing except, very faint, an echo of my own useless words.

I lurched to my feet, reaching for the anger, cloaking myself in it. Not-Too sprang to her feet and backed away from me.

"What to do now? What bloody fucking hell to do *now*?"

Still nothing, but Not-Too started back down the empty corridor. I was glad to transfer my anger to something visible, real, living. "There's nothing there, Not-Too. *Nothing*, you stupid dog!"

She stopped halfway down the corridor and began to scratch at the wall.

I stumbled along behind her, one hand clamped to my head. What the hell was she doing? This piece of wall was identical to every other piece of wall. Kneeling slowly—it hurt my head to move fast—I studied Not-Too. Her scratching increased in frenzy and her nose twitched, as if she smelled something. The wall, of course, didn't respond; nothing in this place responded to anything. Except—

Blue had learned words from me, had followed my commands. Or had he just transferred my command to the Dome's unimaginable machinery, instructing it to do anything I said that fell within permissible limits? Feeling like an idiot, I said to the wall, "Make garbage." Maybe if it complied and the garbage contained food . . .

The wall made no garbage. Instead it dissolved into the familiar gray fog, and Not-Too immediately jumped through, barking frantically.

Every time I had gone through a Dome wall, my situation had gotten worse. But what other choices were there? Wait for Blue to find and kill me, starve to death, curl up and die in the heart of a mechanical alien mini-world I didn't understand.

Not-Too's barking increased in pitch and volume. She was terrified or excited or thrilled . . . How would I know? I pushed through the gray fog.

Another gray metal room, smaller than Blue had made my prison but with the same kind of cages against the far wall. Not-Too saw me and raced from the cages to me. Blue floated toward me . . . No, not Blue. This metal sphere was dull green, the color of shady moss. It said, "No human comes into this area."

"Guess again," I said and grabbed the trailing end of Not-Too's rope. She'd jumped up on me once and then had turned to dash back to the cages.

"No human comes into this area," Green repeated. I waited to see what the robot would do about it. Nothing.

Not-Too tugged on her rope, yowling. From across the room came answering barks, weirdly off. Too uneven in pitch, with a strange undertone. Blood, having saturated my makeshift bandage, once again streamed into my eyes. I swiped at it with one hand, turned to keep my gaze on Green, and let Not-Too pull me across the floor. Only when she stopped did I turn to look at the mesh-topped cages. Vertigo swooped over me.

Mangy was the source of the weird barks, a Mangy altered not beyond recognition but certainly beyond anything I could have imagined. Her mange was gone, along with all her fur. The skin beneath was now gray, the same gunmetal gray as everything else in the Dome. Her ears, the floppy poodle ears, were so long they trailed on the floor of her cage, and so was her tail. Holding on to the tail was a gray grub.

Not a grub. Not anything Earthly. Smooth and pulpy, it was about the size of a human head and vaguely oval. I saw no openings on the thing, but Mangy's elongated tail disappeared into the doughy mass, so there must have been at least one orifice. As Mangy jumped at the bars, trying to get at Not-Too, the grub was whipped back and forth across the cage floor. It left a slimy trail. The dog seemed oblivious.

"This dog is ready," Blue had said.

Behind me Green said, "No human comes into this area."

"Up yours."

"The human does not behave correctly."

That got my attention. I whirled around to face Green, expecting to be vaporized like the dead puppy, the dead Vicious. I thought I was already dead—and then I welcomed the thought. *Look, Mommy, here I am Mommy look . . .* The laws of survival that had protected me for so long couldn't protect me against memory, not any more. I was ready to die.

Instead Mangy's cage dissolved, she bounded out, and she launched herself at me.

Poodles are not natural killers, and this one was small. However, Mangy was doing her level best to destroy me. Her teeth closed on my arm. I screamed and shook her off, but the next moment she was biting my leg above my boot, darting hysterically toward and away from me, biting my legs at each lunge. The grub, or whatever it was, lashed around at the end of her new tail. As I flailed at the dog with both hands, my bandage fell off. Fresh blood from my head wound blinded me. I stumbled and fell and she was at my face.

Then she was pulled off, yelping and snapping and howling.

Not-Too had Mangy in her jaws. Twice as big as the poodle, she shook Mangy violently and then dropped her. Mangy whimpered and rolled over on her belly. Not-Too sprinted over to me and stood in front of me, skinny legs braced and scrawny hackles raised, growling protectively.

Dazed, I got to my feet. Blood, mine and the dogs', slimed everything. The floor wasn't trying to reabsorb it. Mangy, who'd never really liked me, stayed down with her belly exposed in submission, but she didn't seem to be badly hurt. The grub still latched onto the end of her tail like a gray tumor. After a moment she rolled onto her feet and began to nuzzle the grub, one baleful eye on Not-Too: *Don't you come near this thing*! Not-Too stayed in position, guarding me.

Green said—and I swear its mechanical voice held satisfaction, no one will ever be able to tell me any different—"These dogs behave correctly."

The other cages held grubs, one per cage. I reached through the front bars and gingerly touched one. Moist, firm, repulsive. It didn't respond to my touch, but Green did. He was beside me in a flash. "No!"

"Sorry." His tone was dog-disciplining. "Are these the masters?"

No answer.

"What to do now? One dog for one . . ." I waved at the cages.

"Yes. When these dogs are ready."

This dog is ready, Blue had said of Mangy just before she was tumbled into the floor. Ready to be a pet, a guardian, a companion, a service animal to alien . . . what? The most logical answer was "children." Lassie, Rin Tin Tin, Benji, Little Guy. A boy and his dog. The aliens found humans dangerous or repulsive or uncaring or whatever, but dogs . . . You could count on dogs for your kids. Almost, and for the first time, I could see the point of the Domes.

"Are the big masters here? The adults?"

No answer.

"The masters are not here," I said. "They just set up the Domes as . . . as nurseries-slash-obedience schools." And to that statement I didn't even expect an answer. If the adults had been present, surely one or more would have come running when an alien blew into its nursery wing via a garbage delivery. There would have been alarms or something. Instead, there was only Blue and Green and whatever bots inhabited whatever place held the operating room. Mangy's skin and ears and tail had been altered to fit the needs of these grubs. And maybe her voice box, too, since her barks now had that weird undertone, like the scrape of metal across rock. Somewhere there was an OR.

I didn't want to be in that somewhere.

Green seemed to have no orders to kill me, which made sense because he wasn't programmed to have me here. I wasn't on his radar, which raised other problems.

"Green, make bread."

Nothing.

"Make water."

Nothing.

But two indentations in a corner of the floor, close to a section of wall, held water and dog-food pellets. I tasted both, to the interest of Not-Too and the growling of Mangy. Not too bad. I scooped all the rest of the dog food out of the trough. As soon as the last piece was out, the wall filled it up again. If I died, it wasn't going to be of starvation.

A few minutes ago, I had wanted to die. *Zack* . . .

No. Push the memory away. Life was shit, but I didn't want death, either. The realization was visceral, gripping my stomach as if that organ had been laid in a vise, or . . . There is no way to describe it. The feeling just was, its own justification. I wanted to live.

Not-Too lay a short distance away, watching me. Mangy was back in her cage with the grub on her tail. I sat up and looked around. "Green, this dog is not ready."

"No. What to do now?"

Well, that answered one question. Green was programmed to deal with dogs, and you didn't ask dogs "what to do now." So

Green must be in some sort of communication with Blue, but the communication didn't seem to include orders about me. For a star-faring advanced race, the aliens certainly weren't very good at LANs. Or maybe they just didn't care—how would I know how an alien thinks?

I said, "I make this dog behave correctly." The all-purpose answer.

"Yes."

Did Green know details—that Not-Too refused to pull me from oily pools and thus was an obedience-school failure? It didn't seem like it. I could pretend to train Not-Too—I could actually train her, only not for water rescue—and stay here, away from the killer Blue, until . . . until what? As a survival plan, this one was shit. Still, it followed Laws #1 and #3: Take what you can get and never volunteer. And I couldn't think of anything else.

"Not-Too," I said wearily, still shaky from my crying jag, "Sit."

***

"Days" went by, then weeks. Not-Too learned to beg, roll over, bring me a piece of dog food, retrieve my thrown boot, lie down, and balance a pellet of dog food on her nose. I had no idea if any of these activities would be useful to an alien, but as long as Not-Too and I were "working," Green left us alone. No threats, no presentations, no objections. We were behaving correctly. I still hadn't thought of any additional plan. At night I dreamed of Zack and woke in tears, but not with the raging insanity of my first day of memory. Maybe you can only go through that once.

Mangy's grub continued to grow, still fastened onto her tail. The other grubs looked exactly the same as before. Mangy growled if I came too close to her, so I didn't. Her grub seemed to be drying out as it got bigger. Mangy licked it and slept curled around it and generally acted like some mythical dragon guarding a treasure box. Had the aliens bonded those two with some kind of pheromones I couldn't detect? I had no way of knowing.

Mangy and her grub emerged from their cage only to eat, drink, or shit, which she did in a far corner. Not-Too and I used the same corner, and all our shit and piss dissolved odorlessly into the floor. Eat your heart out, Thomas Crapper.

As days turned into weeks, flesh returned to my bones. Not-Too also lost her starved look. I talked to her more and more, her watchful silence preferable to Green's silence or, worse, his inane and limited repertoires of answers. *"Green, I had a child named Zack. He was shot in the War. He was five." "This dog is not ready."*

Well, none of us ever are.

Not-Too started to sleep curled against my left side. This was a problem because I thrashed in my sleep, which woke her, so she growled, which woke me. Both of us became sleep-deprived and irritable. In the camp, I had slept twelve hours a day. Not much else to do, and sleep both conserved energy and kept me out of sight. But the camp was becoming distant in my mind. Zack was shatteringly vivid, with my life before the war, and the Dome was vivid, with Mangy and Not-Too and a bunch of alien grubs. Everything in between was fading.

Then one "day"—after how much time? I had no idea—Green said, "This dog is ready."

My heart stopped. Green was going to take Not-Too to the hidden OR, was going to— "No!"

Green ignored me. But he also ignored Not-Too. The robot floated over to Mangy's cage and dissolved it. I stood and craned my neck for a better look.

The grub was hatching.

Its "skin" had become very dry, a papery gray shell. Now it cracked along the top, parallel to Mangy's tail. She turned and regarded it quizzically, this thing wriggling at the end of her very long tail but didn't attack or even growl. Those must have been some pheromones.

Was I really going to be the first and only human to see a Dome alien?

I was not. The papery covering cracked more and dropped free of the dog's tail. The thing inside wiggled forward, crawling out like a snake shedding its skin. It wasn't a grub but it clearly wasn't a sentient being, either. A larva? I'm no zoologist. This creature was as gray as everything else in the Dome but it had legs, six, and heads, two. At least, they might have been heads. Both had various indentations. One "head" crept forward, opened an orifice, and fastened itself back onto Mangy's tail. She continued to gaze at it. Beside me, Not-Too growled.

I whirled to grab frantically for her rope. Not-Too had no alterations to make her accept this *thing* as anything other than a small animal to attack. If she did—

I turned just in time to see the floor open and swallow Not-Too. Green said again, "This dog is ready," and the floor closed.

"No! Bring her back!" I tried to pound on Green with my fists. He bobbed in the air under my blows. "Bring her back! Don't hurt her! Don't . . ." do what?

Don't turn her into a nursemaid for a grub, oblivious to me.

Green moved off. I followed, yelling and pounding. Neither one, of course, did the slightest good. Finally I got it together enough to say, "When will Not-Too come back?"

"This human does not behave correctly."

I looked despairingly at Mangy. She lay curled on her side, like a mother dog nursing puppies. The larva wasn't nursing, however. A shallow trough had appeared in the floor and filled with some viscous glop, which the larva was scarfing up with its other head. It looked repulsive.

Law #4: Notice everything.

"Green . . . okay. Just . . . okay. When will Not-Too come back here?"

No answer; what does time mean to a machine?

"Does the other dog return here?"

"Yes."

"Does the other dog get a . . ." A what? I pointed at Mangy's larva.

No response. I would have to wait.

But not, apparently, alone. Across the room another dog tumbled, snarling, from the same section of wall I had once come through. I recognized it as one of the nineteen left in the other room, a big black beast with powerful looking jaws. It righted itself and charged at me. There was no platform, no place to hide.

"No! Green, no, it will hurt me! This dog does not behave—"

Green didn't seem to do anything. But even as the black dog leapt toward me, it faltered in midair. The next moment, it lay dead on the floor.

The moment after that, the body disappeared, vaporized.

My legs collapsed under me. That was what would happen to me if I failed in my training task, was what had presumably happened to the previous two human failures. And yet it wasn't fear that made me sit so abruptly on the gray floor. It was relief, and a weird kind of gratitude. Green had protected me, which was more than Blue had ever done. Maybe Green was brighter, or I had proved my worth more, or in this room as opposed to the other room, all dog-training equipment was protected. I was dog-training equipment. It was stupid to feel grateful.

I felt grateful.

Green said, "This dog does not—"

"I know, *I know*. Listen, Green, what to do now? Bring another dog here?"

"Yes."

"*I* choose the dog. I am the . . . the dog leader. Some dogs behave correctly, some dogs do not behave correctly. I choose. Me."

I held my breath. Green considered, or conferred with Blue, or consulted its alien and inadequate programming. Who the hell knows? The robot had been created by a race that preferred Earth dogs to whatever species usually nurtured their young, if any did. Maybe Mangy and Not-Too would replace parental care on the home planet, thus introducing the idea of babysitters. All I wanted was to not be eaten by some canine nanny-trainee.

"Yes," Green said finally, and I let out my breath.

A few minutes later, eighteen dog cages tumbled through the wall like so much garbage, the dogs within bouncing off their bars and mesh tops, furious and noisy. Mangy jumped, curled more protectively around her oblivious larva, and added her weird, rock-scraping bark to the din. A cage grew up around her. When the cages had stopped bouncing, I walked among them like some kind of tattered lord, choosing.

"This dog, Green." It wasn't the smallest dog but it had stopped barking the soonest. I hoped that meant it wasn't a grudge holder. When I put one hand into its cage, it didn't bite me, also a good sign. The dog was phenomenally ugly, the jowls on its face drooping from small, rheumy eyes into a sort of folded ruff around its short neck. Its body that seemed to be all front, with stunted and short back legs. When it stood, I saw it was male.

"This dog? What to do now?"

"Send all the other dogs back."

The cages sank into the floor. I walked over to the feeding trough, scooped up handfuls of dog food, and put the pellets into my only pocket that didn't have holes. "Make all the rest of the dog food go away."

It vaporized.

"Make this dog's cage go away."

I braced myself as the cage dissolved. The dog stood uncertainly on the floor, gazing toward Mangy, who snarled at him. I said, as commandingly as possible, "Ruff!"

He looked at me.

"Ruff, come."

To my surprise, he did. Someone had trained this animal before. I gave him a pellet of dog food.

Green said, "This dog behaves correctly."

"Well, I'm really good," I told him, stupidly, while my chest tightened as I thought of Not-Too. The aliens, or their machines, did understand about anesthesia, didn't they? They wouldn't let her suffer too much? I would never know.

But now I *did* know something momentous. I had choices. I had chosen which room to train dogs in. I had chosen which dog to train. I had some control.

"Sit," I said to Ruff, who didn't, and I set to work.

Not-Too was returned to me three or four "days" later. She was gray and hairless, with an altered bark. A grub hung onto her elongated tail, undoubtedly the same one that had vanished from its cage while I was asleep. But unlike Mangy, who'd never liked either of us, Not-Too was ecstatic to see me. She wouldn't stay in her grub-cage against the wall but insisted on sleeping curled up next to me, grub and all. Green permitted this. I had become the alpha dog.

Not-Too liked Ruff, too. I caught him mounting her, her very long tail conveniently keeping her grub out of the way. Did Green understand the significance of this behavior? No way to tell.

We settled into a routine of training, sleeping, playing, eating. Ruff turned out to be sweet and playful but not very intelligent, and training took a long time. Mangy's grub grew very slowly, considering the large amount of glop it consumed. I grew, too; the waistband of my ragged pants got too tight and I discarded them, settling for a loin cloth, shirt, and my decaying boots. I talked to the dogs, who were much better conversationalists than Green since two of them at least pricked up their ears, made noises back at me, and wriggled joyfully at attention. Green would have been a dud at a cocktail party.

I don't know how long this all went on. Time began to lose meaning. I still dreamed of Zack and still woke in tears, but the dreams grew gentler and farther apart. When I cried, Not-Too crawled onto my lap, dragging her grub, and licked my chin. Her brown eyes shared my sorrow. I wondered how I had ever preferred the disdain of cats.

Not-Too got pregnant. I could feel the puppies growing inside her distended belly.

"Puppies will be easy to make behave correctly," I told Green, who said nothing. Probably he didn't understand. Some people need concrete visuals in order to learn.

Eventually, it seemed to me that Ruff was almost ready for his own grub. I mulled over how to mention this to Green but before I did, everything came to an end.

Clang! Clang! Clang!

I jerked awake and bolted upright. The alarm—a very human-sounding alarm—sounded all around me. Dogs barked and howled. Then I realized that it was a human alarm, coming from the Army camp outside the Dome, on the opposite side to the garbage dump. I could *see* the camp—in outline and faintly, as if through heavy gray fog. The Dome was dissolving.

"Green—what—no!"

Above me, transforming the whole top half of what had been the Dome, was the bottom of a solid saucer. Mangy, in her cage, floated upwards and disappeared into a gap in the saucer's underside. The other grub cages had already disappeared. I glimpsed a flash of metallic color through the gap: Blue. Green was halfway to the opening, drifting lazily upward. Beside me, both Not-Too and Ruff began to rise.

"No! No!"

I hung onto Not-Too, who howled and barked. But then my body froze. I couldn't move anything. My hands opened and Not-Too rose, yowling piteously.

"No! No!" And then, before I knew I was going to say it, "Take me, too!"

Green paused in midair. I began babbling.

"Take me! Take me! I can make the dogs behave correctly—I can—you need me! Why are you going? Take me!"

"Take this human?"

Not Green but Blue, emerging from the gap. Around me the Dome walls thinned more. Soldiers rushed toward us. Guns fired.

"Yes! What to do? Take this human! The dogs want this human!"

Time stood still. Not-Too howled and tried to reach me. Maybe that's what did it. I rose into the air just as Blue said, "Why the hell not?"

Inside—inside *what*?—I was too stunned to do more than grab Not-Too, hang on, and gasp. The gap closed. The saucer rose.

After a few minutes, I sat up and looked around. Gray room, filled with dogs in their cages, with grubs in theirs, with noise and confusion and the two robots. The sensation of motion ceased. I gasped, "Where . . . where are we going?"

Blue answered. "Home."

"*Why*?"

"The humans do not behave correctly." And then, "What to do now?"

We were leaving Earth in a flying saucer, and it was asking *me*?

Over time—I have no idea how much time—I actually got some answers from Blue. The humans "not behaving correctly" had apparently succeeding in breaching one of the Domes somewhere. They must have used a nuclear bomb, but that I couldn't verify. Grubs and dogs had both died, and so the aliens had packed up and left Earth. Without, as far as I could tell, retaliating. Maybe.

If I had stayed, I told myself, the soldiers would have shot me. Or I would have returned to life in the camp, where I would have died of dysentery or violence or cholera or starvation. Or I would have been locked away by whatever government still existed in the cities, a freak who had lived with aliens, none of my story believed. I barely believed it myself.

I *am* a freak who lives with aliens. Furthermore, I live knowing that at any moment Blue or Green or their "masters" might decide to vaporize me. But that's really not much different from the uncertainty of life in the camp, and here I actually have some status. Blue produces whatever I ask for, once I get him to understand what that is. I have new clothes, good food, a bed, paper, a sort of pencil.

And I have the dogs. Mangy still doesn't like me. Her larva hasn't as yet done whatever it will do next. Not-Too's grub grows slowly, and now Ruff has one, too. Their three puppies are adorable and very trainable. I'm not so sure about the other seventeen dogs, some of whom look wilder than ever after their long confinement in small cages. Aliens are not, by definition, humane.

I don't know what it will take to survive when, and if, we reach "home" and I meet the alien adults. All I can do is rely on Jill's Five Laws of Survival:

#1: Take what you can get.

#2: Show no fear.

#3: Never volunteer.

#4: Notice everything.

But the Fifth Law has changed. As I lie beside Not-Too and Ruff, their sweet warmth and doggie-odor, I know that my first formulation was wrong. "Feel nothing"—that can take you some ways toward survival, but not very far. Not really.

Law #5: Take the risk. Love something.

The dogs whuff contentedly and we speed toward the stars.

"Books Cannot Be Sold as Though They're John Deere Tractors"

Nancy Kress Interviewed by Nick Mamatas

Oddly enough, the first question in the last Outspoken Author interview Terry Bisson ever completed is also the first question in my first interview: Ever go back to Buffalo?

Yes, my brother lives near there and since my father died, his house is the gathering point on holidays for the family, so I'm back there every Christmas. This Christmas it looks a little complicated because just last week a tornado went through Buffalo, which Buffalo never gets, and a large tree landed on his house. A lot of trees landed on a lot of houses, so the city hasn't yet removed it. It's settling on the roof, and the doors are getting a little hard to open, so we will see what happens. My children are settled in Rochester, so I go to Rochester a lot.

You were a copywriter, and for a company founded by an author, the mystery writer and fantasist Mary Stanton? Do the skills of copywriting inform your craft at all?

No. They are two different modes of writing, and I never intended to make a career of either. I was a fourth-grade teacher, then I married and had kids and dropped out of the working world for a while. I began writing fiction while raising the kids. My first husband and I divorced while I was also teaching at a college—not on the tenure track, just covering for classes—and suddenly I was a divorced mother in America who needed to find a real job, preferably one I could do from home.

I was teaching a one-week creative writing workshop jointly with Fred Pohl, and Mary took my class. She offered me a job copywriting. I told her that I knew nothing about copywriting but she said she would teach me. I worked with her for several years, mostly writing copy for Xerox. My priorities were number one, my kids, number two, my own writing, and number three Xerox, but since Xerox was satisfied with my work, presumably they never knew they'd come in third.

Regarding "Patent Infringement," your 2002 story about a kind of flu and a vaccine that involved gene insertion, how does it feel to accurately predict the future? Is it cool, is it scary, can we go to Emerald Downs and place some bets after this?
I predicted it a lot better in my novella *Yesterday's Kin*, in which aliens arrive and demand to speak to the United Nations. They have come to warn humanity about a cloud of space-based spores that have already decimated two worlds. Geneticists, biologists, and politicians of people are gathered in New York to start work on a vaccine, and they have less than a year before the spores arrive. I did a lot of research on vaccine development, and *Yesterday's Kin* won a Nebula Award, so I guess I was convincing. This was all before COVID, but for decades epidemiologists had been saying we were overdue for a global pandemic, so I was hardly prescient. You should find somebody else to place your bets at Emerald Downs.

Same question, but about "Product Development" and the ubiquity of the smartphone and the collapse of pretty much other social formation.
Oh, that was already happening, but with computers and the internet. Kids were already using the internet all the time, so it

wasn't really predictive, but a satire. It's a very short piece, under a thousand words, that I wrote for *Nature*, the scientific journal. I don't normally write such short pieces.

How do you research your SF, especially the genetics and biochemistry? If I recall correctly, you once wrote that you never took chemistry in high school.

Yes, I didn't take chemistry in high school, but I am highly interested in genetics. Genetic engineering is not only the future, it is the *now*. I research heavily, and I subscribe to a magazine called *Science News*, a biweekly magazine that publishes brief articles about recent scientific developments. If I find something interesting, I start by researching online, and then I reach out to specialists. I collect microbiologists the same way some people collect butterflies. Just one example: For a story called "Computer Virus," I needed to know what made a virus turn airborne. Three emails to microbiologists brought me one with a detailed, clear, factual description that was exactly what I needed.

You like to write long: that is, novellas, novelettes, novels and even series. But you have written a few pieces that are very short, and you've never written the enormous seven-hundred-page monster. Do you tend to know, when you have an idea, or even when you start composing, how long a story will end up?

The novella is my favorite length; it is long enough to develop an alternative world or alternative future, but you can shoot the plot straight through, without needing to develop subplots. I rarely write short flash fictions; a four-thousand-word story is on the short side for me. But you can't really make a living writing novellas.

You've also expanded novellas into novels and even series. Is that something you plan in advance, using novellas as a test run, or due to fan demands or publisher solicitations or just plain for fun or what?
No, it's not the fans or publishers for the most part. I may just return to a world or to a story because I have something more to say. One exception was the third *Beggars* novel. *Beggars in Spain* started as a novella, and I expanded it into a novel, and then wrote the sequel, *Beggars and Choosers.* I wanted Tor Books to publish my short story collection, and they didn't want to, since short story collections usually don't sell. I also had a thriller I wanted them to publish, and they didn't want to do that, either. So my agent, Ralph Vicinanza, brought me down to New York to have lunch with Tom Doherty and David Hartwell to reach some sort of solution. It was a very nice lunch. We didn't discuss business until dessert.

At dessert Tom said that he would publish my collection and my thriller as part of a three-book deal if I agreed to joint accounting* tied with my third book in the *Beggars* series. I said, "*What* third book in the *Beggars* series?" and Ralph kicked me under the table. And then I said, "Oh yes, the third book!" Tom asked me what my ideas were for it, and I started spouting ideas off the top of my head. I wasn't even keeping track of what I was saying, but whatever I said was persuasive, and I got that three-book deal.

If you didn't have to sleep at all, what would you do with yourself for those extra eight or ten hours?
What wouldn't I do! I'd read more. I'd take long walks. I'd quilt. I would learn more about chess; I'm fascinated with chess but am

---

* Joint accounting means that all books in a multibook deal must "earn out" or make their advance money back for the author to see royalty payments.

not a very good player. I would travel more. And, of course, I'd write more. I've always regretted not going to law school. I'm too old for that now, but if I'd never had to sleep, perhaps I could have become a lawyer, along with fiction writer and mother. Unless, of course, my children didn't sleep either, and then I'd have been screwed.

Headlines frequently appear in your stories, including tabloid-style ones such as "Sleepless Mutie Begs for Reversal of Gene Tampering" in Beggars in Spain *and "'My Twin Sons Were Fathered by the Object' Claims Senator's Daughter, Resists DNA Testing (Polls Show 46% of Americans Believe Her)" in your story "Savior." And these tabloid headlines are often juxtaposed with the less bombastic ones you might read in an upmarket broadsheet. Do you have a special interest in print journalism, or in the sort of movies from, say the 1940s and '50s, that would send headlines spiraling at the viewer?*

Oh, I don't actually like films from the 1940s and '50s— the actors tend to overact, and I am not a fan of black-and-white movies. But I do use headlines frequently. The use of headlines has two advantages: one is that you can deliver a lot of information to the reader very efficiently without depending on a lot of "As you know, Bob" dialogue, where the characters spend pages explaining things to one another.

The second is that tabloid headlines are so ridiculous and you can have a lot of fun with them. I love reading the headlines at the supermarket. The best actual tabloid headline I ever read was "Coca-Cola Addicted Woman Gives Birth to Sugar-Coated Baby."

Terry Bisson used to ask every Outspoken Author what they drove, but Terry was also a gifted mechanic and a total gearhead. I, on the other hand, don't even have a license. What do you drive? Feel free to lie; I have no way of discerning the truth.

I don't really care what I drive. I'm pretty much obsessive-compulsive about neatness in my home, but my cars have always been messy because I don't care about them. My son once asked me why my car was so cluttered when the house is so neat, and I explained to him that the car is just a moving extension of the yard. I don't do yard work.

Jack [Skillingstead, Nancy's husband and a SF author in his own right] is in love with our car. For a long time we had a simple Honda Fit, but recently we upgraded to a Honda CR-V. I put a number of scratches and minor dents in our previous car, but I rarely drive the new one because I'm too afraid I'll dent it.

You recently co-wrote a novel, Observer, *with Robert Lanza, an MD and stem-cell researcher. It's a thriller that serves as a vehicle for his theory of biocentrism, which to oversimplify is the claim that conscious perception creates the universe. How did this project come about, and how much of the heavy lifting did you do?*

Dr. Robert Lanza is a leader in genetics and in in biotech; in 2014 he was named by *Time* magazine one of the world's hundred most influential people. We came together via an agency that connects writers to politicians and other figures who want to write a book. For the most part the agency works with nonfiction writers, but in this case Bob wanted to write a novel to popularize the idea of biocentrism. I read all three of Bob's nonfiction titles on biocentrism and found his ideas intriguing. I won't say I buy into all of it, but I have always believed that consciousness plays an important role in the universe.

Hard SF is always, or should always be, about scientific theory as a jumping-off point for speculation. I was well-positioned to write a story using Bob's ideas as that jumping-off point, but the characters, their individual stories, and the actual prose are all mine. Bob and I developed the general plot together as I wrote the book. I would send him the newest chapters and we'd go over them, with him suggesting modifications to how I had presented the science.

Are you a biocentrist? Should I be a biocentrist?
I think there is a connection between consciousness and the universe. I'll go that far. As for what *you* should be, don't ask me!

You used to teach at the Clarion workshop fairly frequently. What's the single best craft tip or bit of writing advice you can give to someone who cannot spare the six weeks away from their everyday lives to attend?
Up until this year, which is 2024, my advice would be to attend Taos Toolbox, which I teach with Walter John Williams every year in Albuquerque, New Mexico, and that's only two weeks long. However, this year was our final year. I've done it for thirteen years, he did it for fifteen, and it went well. Now I'd recommend finding another workshop that is shorter than Clarion or Odyssey (also six weeks). Viable Paradise, for example, is only one week long.

The important thing about a good workshops is that it provides you with instructors who are working SF professionals, and also with other students to provide reader feedback. Plus, of course, to have a potentially awesome time with.

But many, perhaps even most, successful writers never attended workshops at all. The best advice is still the hardest: write, read, write some more, keep an open mind about what feedback you do get, and write again.

Back when I was coediting Clarkesworld, *I'd frequently receive stories from recent Clarion alumni who either in their cover letters or sometimes even in their rejections, assured me that Nancy Kress said their story was good. Did you know that people do this sort of thing?*

Oh, you edited *Clarkesworld*?

Years ago!
It must have been years ago; I haven't taught Clarion since 2008.

Yes, that was when I was editing the magazine.
I do tell students to note on their cover letters that their submissions were workshopped at Clarion or Taos or wherever; I think that helps. Does it?

Yes, it's just not helpful when they tell me in response to rejection! So, read anything good lately?
One book I read recently that was both excellent and dangerous was *Babel, or the Necessity of Violence* by R.F. Kuang. It was extremely interesting, very well-written, and had a lot to say, but its plot, like its subtitle, is a justification for political violence, which I consider dangerous.

Another traditional, good novel I read recently was *Station Eleven* by Emily St. John Mandel. A book—not often considered SF but really is—and that I liked a lot was *Life After Life* by Kate Atkinson. It's superb, and this was the second time I read it. Right now I am reading the decidedly nontraditional, weirdly wonderful *Lincoln in the Bardo*, by George Saunders.

I think PM Press readers would especially be interested in Beggars in Spain, *which tangles with both a left-anarchism and a right-wing Objectivist-inflected oligarchy. How did that theme emerge in the writing, and now, thirty years later where we have seen both powerful anarchist-informed movements such as Occupy and members of Congress waving around copies of* Atlas Shrugged *like it's the Bible, what would be the way forward?*

Ayn Rand annoys me a lot because in *Atlas Shrugged* she doesn't even hold true to her own principles. In her kind of ideal anarchy, there are no children, no families, no badly aged or seriously disabled relatives—since the only moral position is to be out for yourself entirely. But that is impossible with real, dependent bodies. And she doesn't even stick with that. There are all of two children in all of *Atlas Shrugged*, and their mother declares that the children are her "project." Everyone in Galt's Gulch has some project, but Rand says that one can never make anyone else their project, the center of their life, so by having this character say her children are that, Rand is subverting her own principle.

My favorite SF novel of all time is *The Dispossessed* by Ursula K. Le Guin, and that is a working anarchy. But it is only a working anarchy because the society is on a moon, distant from other societies, and children are raised from birth to believe in and live in the anarchy, and language was changed to eliminate talking about ownership and possessions. But even then, there is still some hierarchy, authority, a committee that makes decisions. The physics department where Shevek works is clearly hierarchical, just like academic departments here on Earth. Le Guin was too smart to believe that one can have a total, perfect anarchy.

Terry also liked to offer a stimulus of three words or phrases to get instant reactions, so I'll carry on the tradition: Sicily, mRNA, nuclear family.
Sicily is where my mother's family was from. My grandfather could not read or write in any language. I wish we could have hung on to more of the culture and the language over the course of generations. All we have left is a box full of recipes and a collection of very inventive curses in dialect.

mRNA is messenger RNA, which reminds me of *Codebreaker*, a biography of geneticist Jennifer Doudna, who led one of the teams that developed the COVID vaccine.

Nuclear family is one kind of family. There are other kinds of families, and all are valid. There are families with same-sex parents, "friend families" where there are no blood relations, extended families, blended families, more. We need a society where all kinds of families are accepted.

This is my first interview, so I want to create my own question that I'll ask every Outspoken Author from now on: If you could change one and only one thing about the publishing industry, what would it be, and why?

I would change the publishing industry to focus on cultivating the midlist. John Irving wrote *Setting Free the Bears*, *The Water-Method Man*, and *The 158-Pound Marriage*—these novels each sold fewer than two thousand copies. Then his fourth novel was *The World According to Garp*. Authors are no longer given a chance to grow or to find an audience before publishers drop them for low numbers. I was very lucky in that David Hartwell nurtured my fiction while I developed as a writer. I had the opportunity to find an audience and have a career. Books cannot be sold as though they're John Deere tractors. Trying to do so hurts writers and, in the long run, readers.

Speaking of your career, what are you working on now?

I am finishing a fantasy novel, *The Queen's Witch*, set at the court of Henry VIII. Anne Boleyn, despite rumors among her contemporaries, was not a witch. But in my novel, she has one to whom she is bound in a way that neither woman likes. However, they need each other to reach their very different goals. I am loving writing it.

Finally, a bonus question! Many authors, especially in the SFF field, are cat people and not dog people—what's wrong with them?

I *know*! Something is wrong! Cats are . . . well. I have a dog. Dogs are friendly and loyal, and cute. Look at this picture of my dog, Pippin, the cutest long-haired Chihuahua in existence. It took ten thousand years of canine domestication to produce that little face. Evolution succeeds again.

Amy Lowell, Cixin Liu, Jane Austen, and the Art of Fiction

WHAT DO JANE AUSTEN and Cixin Liu have in common?

On the surface, nothing. Jane Austen wrote stories of romance and Regency society in early nineteenth-century country towns. Cixin Liu is the twenty-first-century, internationally acclaimed author of *The Three-Body Problem*, a novel spanning decades in China, from the Cultural Revolution of the 1960s through a future alien invasion of Earth. But before any explanation of why I mention these two together, I want to begin at a point chronologically halfway between them: 1917.

In that year, Amy Lowell wrote a poem called "Patterns." The poem is about the restrictive patterns of a woman's life and the possibility of breaking those patterns through love. It is a bitter poem, a cry of grief:

> For the man who should loose me is dead,
> Fighting with the Duke in Flanders,
> In a pattern called a war.
> Christ! What are patterns for?

The woman in the poem is not Lowell, who did not lose a soldier lover in World War I; she was gay and had a lifelong relationship with another woman. The poet was commenting on a pattern not her own but dominant in the society of her time. It is a brilliant poem, but like most patterns, it simplifies the story. More on this soon.

Pattern seeking is hardwired into the human brain. It is one of the strongest tools for making sense of the jumble of sensory input that constantly bombards us: from our eyes, our ears, our tactile sense, the screens with which we surround ourselves. The pattern-seeking starts very young. When my son was three or four, he asked, "Mommy, if a scary monster lies down, is it big enough to make a carpet?" Kevin was looking to relate information he had (a carpet lies on the floor and is the size of the rug in his room) to get a fix on the information in his imagination (scary monsters exist). He was trying to create a pattern.

Patterns to organize information underlay our social rituals, our politics, our art. Some of those patterns are joyful. Consider wedding rituals both religious and secular, or the pleasures of holiday customs, or the bonding that occurs at gatherings ranging from childhood bedtime routines to concerts to football games to political rallies. At each, the participants enact prescribed steps organized around shared information.

The problem with patterns arises from that very fact, plus two other facts. First, the shared information may be incorrect or too limited. Second, people who do not embrace a particular socially accepted pattern are outsiders and therefore often are considered inferior. Third, patterns are not static. They change. These three problems apply not only to life but to fiction as well.

Life first:

Consider Galileo Galilei, forced by the Catholic Church to recant his statement that Earth revolves around the sun instead of the other way around. This regrettable incident occurred due to all three pattern problems. The patterns underlaying the Catholic system of beliefs of that era contained incorrect and limited information about astronomy. The pattern eventually changed; today's Catholic belief systems accept the scientific model of the solar system, which makes it fortunate that Galileo was not executed; death is a part of pattern change that can't be undone. But because his model of the solar system did not match the Church's pattern, Galileo was an inferior "heretic," next door to being demonized.

This problem with pattern making persists today, and here is how such demonization works: If I am right on some critical issue, you must be wrong. If I am right, I am therefore (pick one) doing God's work / on the right side of history / acting in a more moral way than you. I am on the side of good. Since you disagree with me on this critical issue, you must be opposed to good and so on the side of evil. And violence to eradicate evil is justified.

If you do not recognize this pattern in our current culture and our current politics as I write this (in the summer of 2024), you are not looking carefully enough. People on all sides of our current cultural and political situation choose the information they will look at, and they choose different information. Some of it is more correct than the rest of it. All of it is limited. And for far too many people, the result is demonization of the other side.

Before I hear howls of protest, let me clarify one crucial point, and then ask you to conduct a thought experiment. The crucial point here is *not* that all sides of any given political question are equally right. Not, not, not. Hitler does not have moral equivalency with Saint Francis of Assisi. The point is that our penchant to create patterns leads us to ignore both the limitations of our own knowledge and to attribute evil intentions to those on the other side of any question, who also have limited knowledge. The point is that wide-scale demonization not only does more harm than good; it also leads to both inaccurate pictures of ourselves and our adversaries.

Why? Partly due to limited information about people on the other side, and partly because patterns change.

Now for the thought experiment.

Your moral position has triumphed. You have fought the good fight and succeeded in fashioning events so that a moral outcome, without too much compromise, has been attained. In fact, you are recognized as a national hero. There are statues made of you, your sayings have been collected into small leather-bound journals, books are written about you. If you can't believe in this—"I'm not the sort of person whom books are written about!"—visualize it anyway. This is a thought experiment. In it, you have been highly instrumental in stopping climate change or restructuring the economy more fairly or making peace in the Middle East or eliminating racism or restoring democracy or whatever your cause may be.

Now 150 years have passed. Most of the country is doing well. Public attention has now been captured in a big way by animal rights. The young—as always—are at the forefront of the fight to give recognition to the dignity and right to life of other species with which we share this planet. Only people guilty of moral ugliness actually eat other conscious species or enslave them for food, clothing, fripperies. It is discovered, through photos and internet records, that not only did you eat beef and bacon, but you actually wore leather shoes and belts and even a jacket, for which an innocent creature had been slaughtered unnecessarily. Wool and cotton and good synthetics had been available, but you participated in the vicious and barbaric custom of wearing other animals' skins to adorn your own. Your statues are pulled down; students protest that a campus building is named after you; you are excoriated in book and song and whatever electronic entertainment exists in that future.

You think this scenario is far-fetched? You think so because the "evil" of wearing leather is not one of today's dominant thought patterns. But 150 years ago, neither were women's right to vote, evolution as a driving biological force, or any sort of economic safety net such as Social Security or Medicare. Patterns change. And you are being judged on one piece of limited if accurate knowledge: that leather coat.

Patterns also change in art, which brings us back to Amy Lowell's poem. It is anti-war, anti-corset, anti–traditional restrictions on women's bodies. All this is good, valid, symbolic of more than is actually included in the poem, and beautifully expressed. But it is not the whole story. Not all wars are as senseless as World War I; not all women dislike wearing corsets and brocade; not all women whose lovers die in war are moored in grief forever. Most, in fact, eventually marry someone else if marriage happens to be what they want. Lowell's poem is an example of fiction simplifying the messy, extremely complex situation that is life in order to impose a pattern on it to create art.

This is what all art does: impose a pattern on life. To do that, a whole lot must be left out. That is not bad, but necessary. Without patterns, there is no art.

Another thought experiment. Write down what you did the first hour after you got out of bed this morning. Every act, every thought, every word spoken. Don't leave anything out: not brushing your teeth, not the quick stray reminder to yourself to buy more bread, not the stairs you descended or the light switch you turned on or the dog you heard barking next door. You will end up with pages and pages of trivia, and it will be boring and chaotic.

Now choose only those details that create a specific mood: that show your depression or trepidation or happiness on this particular day, with at least hints of why this mood exists. Now you have imposed a pattern on events. Now you have the start of a story.

For *Pride and Prejudice*, published in 1813, Jane Austen selected aspects of country living among the English gentry. She left out the war against Napoleon, which had ended the previous year with Waterloo and which had resulted in the deaths of a great many young men. (William Makepeace Thackeray would use this part of reality in *Vanity Fair*.) She left out the lives of the servants at Longbourn, Netherfield, and Pemberley. She left out the far different lives of the peerage under George III, conducted with far different cultural norms. Austen's pattern selection resulted in a wonderful, satiric yet sympathetic, cast of characters who also function as a critique of the society they move in. Her major focus is marriage-as-economic-survival versus marriage-for-love, and she is skillful enough to show that both matter. Her pattern is complex enough to be interesting to a wide range of readers.

Cixin Liu, likewise, creates a pattern in *The Three-Body Problem*. He is concerned with the limits of information, starting with the harrowing first scene (in the English translation by Ken Liu) of a struggle session during the Chinese Cultural Revolution of the 1960s. Young girls, who believe that any "reactionary" act or word brands a person as intending evil toward the state, beat to death a physicist who taught Einstein. Throughout the novel, humans struggle desperately to gain information about their adversaries, aliens who wish to take over Earth. Cixin Liu's pattern is an examination of how we acquire and use information: for good, for advantage, for misguided aims, to self-preservation, for war. He creates complex patterns, by choosing what he includes in his story and what he does not. But it is not, cannot be, the entire story of his characters. We see, for example, the parts of Ye Wenjie's actions that contribute to the novel's pattern, but not other aspects of her life.

All this may seem obvious, but there are implications for the writing of fiction that are worth considering.

First, fiction may fail if the pattern of the story is either too clear or not clear enough. Patterns that are very simple result in readers saying, "I could see the ending coming from page two," or "The characters had the depth of wallpaper," or "The plot is so contrived just to fit the theme." Such books may end up being published, but seldom are they esteemed.

A pattern that is not clear enough either bores readers ("Why is that stuff there—it doesn't seem to have anything to do with the story") or confuses them ("The ending made no sense," or "It didn't add up to anything," or simply "Huh?"). A good novel has a point of view about what happens, even when a lot happens, and even if that point of view is itself complex. In *Anna Karenina*, Anna comes to grief for her scandalous love, while Kitty and Levin flourish for their social-norm-affirming marriage. Is Tolstoy therefore against adultery? Probably, but his pattern is much more complex than that. Anna is a highly sympathetic figure, forced to choose between love and her child. The novel concerns, in addition to romances, patterns about relation to the land, the Church, and the state. Tolstoy has limited and chosen the information he wished to include, but his pattern is neither simplistic nor chaotic.

Fiction, then, is guided by an author's choice of pattern. A story presents a worldview—even the simplest category romance says that "love always conquers all," a patently false but highly comforting pattern. All fiction contrives a story, but the pattern in *good* fiction is not boringly simple because life is not simple and readers want to believe the books they read have some relation to life. Nor is the pattern in good fiction as messy and full as anyone's actual life, because art is not life.

This has implications for critics, too, who too often view all fiction through the lens of their own specific beliefs. In 1891, Thomas Hardy's *Tess of the D'Urbervilles* was published and immediately excoriated as immoral, unfit for publication, and a threat to public morals, because Tess is portrayed, in Hardy's own words, as "more sinned against than sinning." The critics failed to see the novel's genius because it did not conform to their pattern of beliefs about women's ideal behavior. Today, as well, it is not unknown for good fiction to be similarly excoriated for not affirming the critic's belief pattern, whether that be feminism, Marxism, anticolonialism, antidemocratic, in favor or against a strong central state, or half a dozen other beliefs. The questions for critics should be: *Does this ring true? Does it portray a section of life as it exists? Do I believe the characters, their motivations and dilemmas?* Instead, criticism is sometimes written from the question, "Does this affirm how I think the world *should* look, and do so in every minute detail?"

Finally, genre imposes patterns on fiction. This can be both good and bad. It is good when it helps readers locate books with elements they want to read about: space wars or international espionage or witches or love affairs or police procedurals. It is bad when it creates such specific expectations of a genre or subgenre that any novel falling between those patterns, or including two or more patterns from different genres, is not published because publishing houses "don't know how to market it." One of my favorite books, to consider just one example, is Kate Atkinson's 2013 *Life After Life*. The novel is hard to categorize. Is it historical fiction? Yes. Is it fantasy? Yes. Is it feminist? Yes. Is it political? Very. Is it "meta"? Yes. The novel is literary fiction, which basically means that the writing is superior and that it is allowed to cross genre barriers. It helped, too, that British publishing has always been less genre-bound than American publishing. *Brave New World*, *1984*, and *A Clockwork Orange* were all published as simply good novels. American "commercial fiction" is far more restrictive about keeping books in distinct literary categories, and as a result, I know writers who have produced good work that did not sell because "we love it but we wouldn't know how to market it." In that situation, genre becomes a straitjacket.

Patterns, the soul of art, do constrain. They also liberate by shaping the chaotic mess of life into art that at its best moves us, delights us, instructs us in complexities of reality we might not otherwise see. When that happens, patterns expand our world.

As all art should.

Machine Learning

ETHAN SLIPPED INTO THE back of the conference room in Building 5 without being noticed. Fifty researchers and administrators, jammed into the room lab-coat-to-suit, all faced the projection stage. Today, of course, it would be set for maximum display. The CEO of the company was here, his six-foot-three frame looming over the crowd. Beside him, invisible to Ethan in the crush, would be tiny Anne Gonzalez, R&D chief. For five years a huge proportion of the Biological Division's resources—computational, experimental, human—had been directed toward this moment.

Anne's clear voice said, "Run."

Some people leaned slightly forward. Some bit their lips or clasped their hands. Jerry Liu rose onto the balls of his feet, like a fighter. They all had so much invested in this: time, money, hope.

The holostage brightened. The incredibly complex, three-dimensional network of structures within a nerve cell sprang into view, along with the even more complicated lines of the signaling network that connected them. Each line of those networks had taken years to identify, validate, understand. Then more time to investigate how any input to one substructure could change the whole. Then the testing of various inputs, each one a molecule aimed at the deadly thing near the center of the cell, the growing mass of Moser's Syndrome. All this hard work, all the partnering with pharmaceutical companies, in order to arrive at Molecule 654-a, their best chance.

So far, no one had noticed Ethan.

The algorithm for 654-a began to run, and in a moment the interaction combinations produced the output on the right side of the screen. Only two outputs were possible: "continued cell function" or "apoptosis." The apoptosis symbol glowed. A second later, in a burst of nonrealistic theatrics, the cell drooped and sagged like one of Dalí's clocks, and the lethal structure at its heart vanished.

Cheering erupted in the room. People hugged each other. A lab tech stood on tiptoe and kissed the surprised CEO. They had done it, identified a possible cure for the disease that attacked the bodies of children, and only children, killing half a billion kids worldwide in the last five years. They had done it with molecular computation, with worldwide partnerships with universities and Big Pharma, and with sheer grit.

Someone to Ethan's left said, "Oh!" Then someone else noticed him, and someone after that. Ethan's story was companywide gossip. The people at the front of the room went on burbling and hugging, but a small pocket of silence grew around him, the embarrassed silence of people caught giggling at a wake. Laura Avery started toward him.

He didn't want to talk to Laura. He didn't want to spoil this important celebration. Quickly he moved through the door, down the corridor, into the elevator. Laura, following, called, "Ethan!" He hit the DOOR CLOSE button before she could reach him.

In the lobby he walked rapidly out the door, heading in the rain toward his own facility. Buildings of brick and glass rose ghostly in the thick mist. MultiFuture Research was a big campus and he was soaked by the time he reached Building 18. Inside, he nodded at Security and shook himself like a dog. Droplets spun off him. What the hell had he done with his umbrella? He couldn't remember, but it didn't matter. The important thing was to get back to his own work.

He didn't belong at a celebration to defeat Moser's Syndrome.

Too late, too late. Way too late.

* * *

Building 18 was devoted to machine learning. Ethan's research partner, Jamie Peregoy, stood in their lab, welcoming this afternoon's test subject, Cassie McAvoy. The little girl came with her mother every Monday, Wednesday, and Friday after school. Ethan took his place at the display console.

That end of the lab was filled with desks, computers, and messy folders of printouts. The other end held child-sized equipment: a musical keyboard, a video-game console, tables and chairs, blocks, and puzzles. The back wall was painted a supposedly cheerful yellow that Ethan found garish. In the center, like a sentry in no-man's land, stood a table with coffee and cookies.

"The problem with machine learning isn't intelligence," Jamie always said to visitors. "It's *defining* intelligence. Is it intelligence to play superb chess, crunch numbers, create algorithms, carry on a conversation indistinguishable from a human gabfest? No. Turing was wrong. True intelligence requires the ability to learn for oneself, tackling new tasks you haven't done before, and that requires emotion as well as reasoning. We don't retain learning unless it's accompanied by emotion, and we learn best when emotional arousal is high. Can our Mape do that? No, she cannot."

If visitors tried to inject something here, they were out of luck. Jamie would go into full lecture mode, discoursing on the role of the hippocampus in memory retention, on how frontal-lobe injuries taught us that too little emotion could impair decision making as deeply as too much emotion, on how arousal levels were a better predictor of learning retention than whether the learning was positive or negative. Once Jamie got going, he was as unstoppable as a star running back, which was what he resembled. Young, brilliant, and charismatic, he practically glittered with energy and enthusiasm. Ethan went through periods where he warmed himself at Jamie's inner fire, and other periods where he avoided Jamie for days at a time.

MAIP, the MultiFuture Research Artificial Intelligence Program based in the company's private cloud, could not play chess, could not feel emotion, and could only learn within defined parameters. Ethan, whose field was the analysis of how machine learning algorithms performed, believed that true AI was decades off, if ever. Did Jamie believe that? Hard to tell. When he spoke their program's name, Ethan could hear that to Jamie it *was* a name, not an acronym. He had given MAIP a female identity. "Someday," Jamie said, "she'll be smarter than we are." Ethan had not asked Jamie to define "someday."

The immediate, more modest goal was for MAIP to learn what others felt, so that MAIP could better assist their learning.

"Hello, Cassie, Mrs. McAvoy," Jamie said, with one of his blinding smiles. Cassie, a nine-year-old in overalls and a t-shirt printed with kittens, smiled back. She was a prim little girl, eager to please adults. Well-mannered, straight A's, teacher's pet. "Never any trouble at home," her mother had said, with pride. Ethan guessed she was not popular with other kids. But she was a valuable research subject, because MAIP had to learn to distinguish between genuine human emotions and "social pretense"—feelings expressed because convention expected it. When Cassie said, "I like you," did she mean it?

"Ready for the minuet, Cassie?" Jamie asked.

"Yes."

"Then let's get started! Here's your magic bracelet, princess!" He slipped it onto her thin wrist. Mrs. McAvoy took a chair at the back of the lab. Cassie walked to the keyboard and began to play Bach's "Minuet in G," the left-hand part of the arrangement simplified for beginners. Jamie moved behind her, where she could not see him. Ethan studied MAIP's displays.

Sensors in Cassie's bracelet measured her physiological responses: heart rate, blood pressure, respiration, skin conductance, and temperature. Tiny cameras captured her facial-muscle movement and eye saccades. The keyboard was wired to register the pressure of her fingers. When she finished the minuet, MAIP said, "That was good! But let's talk about the way you arch your hands, okay, Cassie?" Voice analyzers measured Cassie's responses: voice quality, timing, pitch. MAIP used the data to adjust the lesson: slowing down her instruction when Cassie seemed too frustrated, increasing the difficulty of what MAIP asked for when the child showed interest.

They moved on, teacher and pupil, to Bach's "Polonaise in D." Cassie didn't know this piece as well. MAIP was responsive and patient, tailoring her comments to Cassie's emotional data.

It looked so effortless. But years of work had gone into this piano lesson between a machine and a not-very-talented child. They had begun with a supervised classification problem, inputting observational data to obtain an output of what a test subject was feeling. Ethan had used a full range of pattern recognition and learning algorithms. But Jamie, the specialist in affective computing, had gone far beyond that. He had built "by hand" one complicated concept at a time, approaches to learning that did not depend on simpler, more general principles like logic. Then he'd made considerable progress in the difficult problem of integrating generative and discriminative models of machine learning. Thanks to Jamie, MAIP was a hybrid, multiagent system, incorporating symbolic and logical components with subsymbolic neural networks, plus some new soft-computing approaches he had invented. These borrowed methods from probability theory to maximize the use of incomplete or uncertain information.

MAIP learned from each individual user. When Cassie's data showed her specific frustration level rising to a point where it interfered with her learning, MAIP slowed down her instruction. When Cassie showed interest in a direction, MAIP took the lesson there. It all looked so smooth, Ethan's and Jamie's work invisible to anyone but them.

At the end of the hour, MAIP said, "Well done, Cassie!"

"Thank you."

"I hope you enjoyed the lesson."

"Yes."

"See you on Monday, then."

"Okay."

Mrs. McAvoy took Cassie's hand, exchanged a few pleasantries with Jamie, and led Cassie out the door. It closed. In the corridor, the motion-activated surveillance system turned on.

Jamie beamed at Ethan. "That went really well! Mape—"

"I don't want to come here anymore," said the image of Cassie on the surveillance screen.

"Why not?" Mrs. McAvoy said.

"It's no fun. Please, Mommy, can we never come here again?"

Silence in the lab. Finally Ethan said, "I guess we need to work more on the ontology of social pretense."

Jamie looked crushed. "Damn! I thought Cassie liked coming here! She fooled me completely!"

"More to the point, she fooled MAIP."

"All the subagents worked so well on yesterday's test kid!"

"There's no free lunch."

Jamie had a rare flash of anger. "Ethan—do you always have to be so negative? And so fucking *calm* about it?"

"Yes," Ethan said, and they parted in mutual snits. Ethan knew that Jamie's wouldn't last; it wasn't in his nature. There they were, yoked together, the Elpis and Cassandra of machine learning.

Or maybe just Roo and Eeyore.

* * *

The first time Ethan had heard about Moser's Syndrome, he'd been chopping wood in the back yard and listening to the news on his tablet. Chopping wood was an anachronism he enjoyed: the warming of his muscles, the satisfying clunk of axe against birch logs, the smell of fresh woodchips on the warm August air. In a corner of the tiny yard, against the whitewashed fence, chrysanthemums bloomed scarlet and gold.

"—coup in Mali that—"

Also, if he was honest with himself, he liked being out of the house while Tina was in it. His year-old marriage was not going well. The vivacity that had originally attracted Ethan, so different from his own habitual constraint, was wearing thin. For Tina, every difference of opinion was a betrayal, every divergent action a crisis. But she was pregnant and Ethan was determined to stick it out.

"—tropical storm off the coast of North Carolina, and FEMA is urging—"

Thunk! Another fall of the axe on wood, not a clean stroke. Ethan pulled the axe out of the log. Tina came out of the house, carrying a tray of iced tea. Although her belly was still flat, she proudly wore a maternity top. The tea tray held a plate of his favorite chocolate macaroons. They were both trying.

"Hey, babes," Tina said. Ethan forced a smile. He'd told her at least three times that he hated being called "babes."

He said, "The cookies look good."

She said, "I hope they are."

The radio said, "Repeat: This just in. The CDC has identified the virus causing Moser's Syndrome, even as the disease has spread to two more cities in the Northwest. Contrary to earlier reports, the disease is transmitted by air and poses a significant threat to fetuses in the first and early second trimester of pregnancy. All pregnant women in Washington and Oregon are urged to avoid public gatherings whenever possible until more is known. The—"

Ethan's axe slipped from his hand, landing on his foot and partially severing his little toe in its leather sandal.

Tina shrieked. In his first stunned moment, he thought she'd screamed at the blood flowing from his foot. But she threw the tray at him, crying, "You took me to that soccer game last week! How *could* you! If anything happens to this baby, I'll never forgive you!" She burst into tears and ran into the house, leaving Ethan staring at the end of his foot. A chunk of toe lay disjointed from the rest, bloody pulp surrounded by chocolate macaroons. Vertigo swept over him. It passed. The newscaster began to interview a doctor about embryonic damage, nerve malformation, visible symptoms in newborns.

Ethan shifted his gaze to the axe, as if it and not a maybe-living-maybe-not molecule was the danger to his unborn child. An ordinary axe: silver blade, hardwood handle, manufacturer's name printed in small letters. Absurdly, a sentence rose in his mind from decades ago, a lecture from his first tech professor when he'd been an undergraduate: *Technology is always double-edged, and the day stone tools were invented, axe murder became possible.*

Then the pain rushed in, and he bent over and vomited. After that, he pushed the chunk of toe back in place, wrapped his shirt around it, and applied pressure.

If anything happens to this baby, I'll never forgive you!

They divorced eighteen months later.

* * *

Social pretense was not a problem with one of Jamie and Ethan's other research subjects, eleven-year-old Trevor Reynod. He barreled into the lab, shouting, "I'm here! Freakish! Let's go!"

"My man!" Jamie said, giving him a fist bump that Trevor practically turned into an assault.

"Jamie! And Dr. Stone Man!" That was the kid's name for Ethan. Ethan didn't object, so long as Trevor stayed well away from him. Trevor had ADHD, though most of the suffering seemed to belong to the tired-looking mother who trailed in after him. A member of some sect that didn't believe in medication, she refused to allow Trevor to be calmed down by drugs, but computer games were apparently allowed. Ethan suspected that these thrice-weekly sessions were an immense relief to her; she could turn Trevor over to someone else. Mrs. Reynod poured herself some coffee and slumped into the easy chair in the corner.

Trevor pummeled the air and danced in place, knocking over a pile of blocks. Jamie got the bracelet onto his wrist ("Your superpower ring, dude!") and settled both of them in front of a game console as carefully wired as Cassie's keyboard. Trevor's data began to flow down Ethan's display. MAIP was silent during Trevor's sessions, adjusting his game in response to his frustration or satisfaction levels but not instructing him. Trevor did not respond well to direct instruction.

The game involved piloting a futuristic one-man plane, ridiculously represented as a bullet-shaped soap bubble. Its flight simulator was state-of-the-art, similar to the one used to train USAF jet pilots, who might eventually have MAIP incorporated into their training sessions. While flying over various war-torn terrains, Trevor had to shoot down alien craft to avoid being vaporized and to dodge "falling stars" that appeared from nowhere. Jamie's role was to fire at Trevor from the ground. He almost never hit him, which allowed MAIP more control and Trevor merciless mockery.

"Ha! Missed me again!"

"You're really good, Trev."

He was. Like most attention-deficit kids, Trevor could muster enormous powers of concentration when the activity actually interested him.

They followed their plan of transitioning Trevor from the shooting game to one teaching math in the last fifteen minutes of the hour. Trevor's levels of arousal and engagement fell, but not as far as they had the previous week. This was a new version of the math game, punchier and more inventive. In effect, Trevor was beta-testing Math Monkeys, while Ethan and Jamie gained learning-algorithm data from him.

The session was a success. After Trevor left, shouting about his victory over the math monkeys, Jamie said, "Did you catch that? Mape tried a stutter-and-recover strategy on him! We didn't program that!"

"Not in quite that form, anyway."

"Come on, Ethan, she figured out for herself how to apply it! She learned!"

"Maybe." He would have to do the analysis first.

But Jamie danced around the lab in an exuberant imitation of Trevor. "Freakish! She did it, Dr. Stone Man! You did it! Go, Mape!"

Ethan smiled. It felt odd, as if his face were cracking.

* * *

At midnight, Ethan let himself into the modeling lab in Building 6. The place was empty, even the most diehard geek having gone out on a Friday night for beer and company. "Lights on low," Ethan said. The lab complied.

He'd told himself he wasn't going to do this again. It only made everything harder. But he could not resist. This was the only place that felt meaningful to him now—or at least the only place where meaning felt natural, like air, instead of having to be manufactured moment after effortful moment.

The lab contained, in addition to its staggeringly expensive machinery, three "rooms," each with the missing fourth wall of a theater stage or a furniture showroom. The largest was an empty, white-walled box, used to project VR environments ranging from an Alpine village to the surface of the moon. The two furnished rooms represented living spaces with sofas and tables, onto which could be projected the VR programs: changing a chair from red velour to yellow brocade, setting out bottles on a table. Old stuff, but it was the starting point for the real challenge of modeling three-dimensional "reality" that could move and be moved, touch and be touched. This lab, already a huge profit-maker for MultiFuture Research, was usually the first one shown to visitors.

Some of the programs, however, were private.

Ethan slipped on a VR glove and put his password into the projector aimed at the smallest room. It sprang to life and Allyson was there, sitting on the floor, holding her stuffed Piglet. This was the Allyson he'd brought to the lab near the end of her illness, after it had become clear that the doctors' pathetically inadequate measures could not help her. Four more months, they said, but it had been only two. Ethan was grateful that Allyson had gone so quickly; he'd seen children for whom Moser's Syndrome took its slower, crueler time.

Tina had not been grateful. By that point, she had barely been Tina.

Allyson had loved Winnie the Pooh. Kanga, Roo, and Eeyore had been her friends, but Piglet had been more: a talisman, an icon. Once she'd told Ethan, "I hate Christopher Robin because *his* Piglet can talk to him and mine can't."

The 3-D model of Allyson raised her head and looked up at Ethan. It was a tremendous technical achievement, that mobile action on a holographic projection. Right now, Ethan didn't care. When he'd brought Allyson here, late at night on another Friday, she'd already begun to lose weight. Her skin had gone as colorless as the sheets she lay on at home. Her hair had fallen out in patches. Ethan had known this was his last chance; the following week Allyson had gone into the hospital. When Tina found out what he'd done, she had raged at him with a ferocity excessive even for her. Although it should have been a warning.

The model of Allyson—or rather, the voice recorder in the computer—said, "Hi, Daddy."

"Hi, baby," Ethan said. And she smiled.

That was it. Ten seconds of Allyson's short life, and an enormous expenditure of bandwidth. He hadn't kept his daughter in the lab longer than that; she'd looked too tired. Ethan hoped that the biological division's molecule 654-a could cure Moser's Syndrome. But for him, there was only this.

He called up the overlay programs, one by one. Allyson's skin brightened to rosy pink. Her hair became thick and glossy again, without bare patches. Her little body grew sturdier. Her eyes opened wider. "Hi, Daddy."

"Hi, baby." He reached out with the VR glove and stroked her cheek. The sensation was there: smooth, warm flesh.

Over and over he played the enhanced, miraculously mobile model. Throughout, Ethan kept his face rigid, his hands under control, his thoughts disciplined. He was not Tina. He would never let himself be Tina.

No one, not friends or colleagues, had known how to treat Ethan after Allyson, after Tina. "Call us," friends had said while Ethan awaited Allyson's diagnosis, "if anything goes wrong." And later, after Tina, "Call us if you need anything." But there is no one to call when everything goes wrong, when you need what you can never have back.

"Hi, Daddy."

"Hi, baby."

When he'd had his fill, the fix that kept him from becoming Tina, he closed the program and went home.

* * *

On Monday, Laura Avery waylaid him as he walked from the parking lot to Building 18. This being October in Seattle, it was still raining, but at least Ethan had remembered his umbrella. She had one, too, blue with a reproduction of a Marc Chagall painting, which seemed to him a frivolous use of great art. Laura, however, was not frivolous. Serious but not humorless, she had made important contributions during her months at MultiFuture Research, or so he'd been told. The company, like all companies, was a cauldron of gossip.

"Ethan! Wait up!"

He had no choice unless he wanted to appear rude.

She was direct, without flirtatious games. Ordinarily he would have liked that. But this was not ordinarily, and never would be again, not for him. Laura said, "I wondered if you'd like to have dinner one night at my place. I'm a good cook, and I can do vegetarian."

"I'm not vegetarian."

"I know, but I thought I'd just show off my fabulous culinary range." She smiled whimsically.

It was an attractive smile; she was an attractive woman. When they'd first been introduced, Laura had glanced quickly at his left hand, and her smile grew warmer. He'd taken off his wedding ring the day after Tina had left him, long before she'd killed herself. Later, after someone had undoubtedly told Laura about Ethan's story, Laura had grown more circumspect. But the warmth had still been there; he hadn't needed MAIP to read her face. Now, a year after Tina's death, this invitation—had someone told Laura it was exactly one year? Was she that coldly correct?

No. She was an intelligent, appealing woman aware enough of her appeal to go directly after someone she liked. Why she liked him was a mystery; in Ethan's opinion, there wasn't enough of him left to like. Or to accept a dinner invitation.

"Sorry. I'm busy."

She recognized the lie but hid any feeling of rejection. "Okay. Maybe another time."

"Thanks anyway."

That was it. A nothing encounter. But it left him feeling fragile, and he hated that. The only thing that had gotten him through the last year was the opposite of fragility: controlled, resolute, carefully modeled action.

After his encounter with Laura, he threw himself into work, trying to figure out why MAIP hadn't detected Cassie McAvoy's social pretense of enjoying her piano lesson. He found a few promising leads, but nothing definitive.

How far they still had to go was made clear by Jenna Carter.

Jamie was good with the children who came to the machine lab. Sometimes Ethan thought this was because Jamie, brilliant as he was, was still a child himself: enthusiastic, sloppy, saved from terminal nerdiness only by his all-American good looks. Untested, as of yet, by anything harsh. Other times Ethan felt ashamed of this facile assessment; Jamie was good with kids because he liked them.

Not, however, all of them equally. While Jamie had no trouble with Trevor Reynod, he had to hide his dislike for Jenna, who wasn't even a test subject, only the babysitter for her little brother Paul.

They came in after school on Tuesday. Paul, at eight years old their youngest subject, went straight to the small table where Jamie had set out a wooden puzzle map of the United States.

"Hey, Paul," Jamie said. "How's it going?"

"Good." Paul had a thin face, a shock of red hair, and a sweet smile.

"Can I put the magic bracelet on you? Have to warn you, though, it might turn you invisible."

Paul looked uncertain for a moment, caught Jamie's grin, and laughed. "No, it won't!"

"Well, if you're sure—let's see if you can put this puzzle together. Recognize it? It's our country, all fifty states. Wow! That's a lot of states! What a challenge!"

"I can do it!"

Jenna pushed forward. "He can't do that! It's too hard! He's only in the third grade!"

"Yes, I can!" Paul picked up Maine and fitted it into the upper right corner of the wooden holder. "See?"

"That one's easy, dingleberry! Anybody can get Maine!" She turned to Jamie. "Our mother said *I* was supposed to do the puzzles today."

Paul looked up, outraged. "No, she didn't!"

"Did too!"

"Did not!" Jenna grabbed her brother by the shoulders and tried to pull him out of the chair.

"Hey! Quit it! Dr. Peregoy!"

Jamie detached Jenna's hands. "Paul, let Jenna try the puzzle. I'll let you do the flight simulator."

Paul's mouth opened and his eyebrows rose: surprise, one of the basic facial-recognition patterns. The flight simulator was a treat usually withheld until the end of each session.

Jenna cried, "No fair! I want to do the flight simulator!"

"Maybe later." Jamie slipped the sensor bracelet off Paul and onto Jenna, then pushed her gently onto the chair. "After all, *your mother* said you should do the puzzle, right?"

Jenna glared at him. "Yeah!"

"Then let's see how fast you can do it."

Jenna hunted for a place to fit Iowa. Paul ineptly piloted the transparent bubble. ("You have crashed the jet, Paul," MAIP said.) Ethan wondered what Jamie was doing. Then he got it: Jamie wanted to see if MAIP could detect the fact that Jenna was lying. Ethan studied his displays.

MAIP worked with what was, basically, a set of medical data. It didn't have the context to interpret what that data might mean. To detect social pretense—which it also couldn't do yet—its algorithms used a subject's baseline data, observed data, and contradictions among the ontologies of emotion. But MAIP hadn't "learned" Jenna, couldn't yet do cold readings without a subject's baseline data, and had neither context nor algorithms to detect lies. It was no surprise that MAIP didn't recognize Jenna's lies.

"Well," Jamie said after the children left, "it was worth a shot."

"Not really," Ethan said.

"Mr. Negative."

"MAIP didn't even register social pretense for Jenna, no matter how much you led her into lying. We're just not there yet."

Jamie sighed. "I know."

"What you just did was no better than a polygraph, and there's a reason polygraphs aren't admissible in court. Not reliable enough."

"Yeah, yeah, you're right. But there should be some way to do this."

"We need to solve the problem of social pretense first, and with subjects that we do have baseline data for."

Jamie said, "Maybe if we . . . No, that wouldn't work. And—oh, God, I just thought of another problem. Jenna clearly knew she was lying, but what if someone has convinced themselves that they feel one thing but are actually feeling something different? Like, say, a woman who convinces herself she's in love, even though all she really wants is to have babies before her biological clock stops ticking? She doesn't really feel love for some poor schlump but thinks she does, to ease her conscience about trapping him?"

Was this a glimpse into Jamie's personal life? If so, Ethan didn't want to know about it. He said, more primly than he intended, "Oh, I think most people know what they really feel."

Jamie gave him a strange look. "Really, Ethan?"

"Yes. But the point here is that MAIP didn't know."

Jamie picked up Texas and fitted it into the puzzle, his head bent over the small table, his hair falling forward over his face and hiding his expression.

* * *

December, and still raining. Ethan went to the modeling lab late on a Sunday afternoon. He was alone in the building; it was almost Christmas. Water dripped from his raincoat and umbrella onto the floor. "Lights on."

"Hi, Daddy."

"Hi, baby."

Allyson smiled, and the recording ended. He clothed her in artificial health, pink cheeks, and lustrous hair, and started it again.

"Hi, Daddy."

"Hi, baby."

He stroked her cheek. Soft, so soft in his VR glove. But Allyson had not been a soft child. Not noisy and obnoxious like Trevor or Jenna, not hidden and falsely polite like Cassie. Allyson had been direct, opinionated, with a will of diamond. She and Tina clashed constantly over what clothes Allyson would put on, what her bedtime was, whether she could cross the street alone, why she drew butterflies instead of the alphabet on her kindergarten "homework." Ethan had been the buffer between his wife and daughter. It seemed ridiculous that a five-year-old had to be buffered against, but that was the way it had been. Allyson and Tina had been too much alike, and when Tina had blamed not only Ethan but herself for exposing Allyson to Moser's Syndrome, Ethan had not seen the danger. Tina, dramatic to the end, had thrown herself under a Metro train at the Westlake Tunnel Station.

Allyson would not have grown up like that. As she matured, she would have become calmer, more controlled. Ethan was sure of it. She would have become the companion and ally that Tina had not been.

"Hi, Daddy."

"Hi, baby."

The recording stopped, but Ethan talked on. "We're having trouble with MAIP's ability to attune, Allyson."

She gazed at him from solemn eyes. Light golden brown, the color of November fields in sunshine.

"'Attune' means that two people are aware of and responsive to each other." And attunement began early, between mother and infant. Was that what had gone wrong between Allyson and Tina? He and Allyson had always been attuned to each other.

Ethan reached out both arms, one in the VR glove and one bare. Both arms passed through the model of Allyson that was made only of light. The gloved hand tingled briefly, but it still moved through the child as if she did not exist.

For a terrible second, Ethan's brain filled with thick, tarry mist, cold as liquid nitrogen. He went rigid and clamped his teeth tightly together. The mist disappeared. He was in control again.

He turned off the recording, wiped the rain droplets from the floor, and left.

* * *

Zhao Tailoring didn't open until 10:00 a.m. on Mondays. Ethan, who'd been there at 8:30, waited in a Starbucks, slowly drinking a latte he didn't want. *The Seattle Times* lay open on the table, but he couldn't concentrate. At 9:50 he threw his paper cup in the trash, left his unread paper, and walked across the street to the tailor shop. He huddled under the roof overhang, out of the rain.

Tailoring was not part of his life. Ethan bought clothes haphazardly, getting whatever size seemed the best fit and ignoring whatever gaps might present themselves. The window of Zhao Tailoring held Christmas decorations and three mannequins. The plastic-resin woman wore a satin gown; the man, slacks and a double-breasted blazer; the child, a pair of overalls over a ruffled blouse. They looked bound for three entirely different events. The sign read ALTERATIONS · REPAIRS · NEW CLOTHES MADE. At 9:58, an Asian woman unlocked the front door.

"Ethan! What are you doing here?"

Laura Avery, under her Marc Chagall umbrella. Ethan felt his face go rigid. "Hello, Laura."

"Are you having tailoring done?" Her voice held amusement but no condescension.

"No. What are you doing here? Why aren't you at work?"

Her brows rose in surprise at his harsh tone. "I had a doctor's appointment across the street. Nothing serious. Are you having a suit made?"

"I already said I wasn't having tailoring done. Please stop asking me personal questions."

Surprise changed to hurt, her features going slack in the blue shadows under the umbrella. "Sorry, I just—"

"If I wanted to talk to you, I would." A moment of silence. Ethan opened his mouth to apologize, to explain that he was just distracted, but before he could speak, she turned and stalked away.

"You come in, yes?" the Asian woman said.

Ethan went in.

"You want nice suit, yes? Special this week."

"No. I don't want a suit. I want . . . I want to buy the mannequin in the window." Incongruously, an old childish song ran through his head: *How much is that doggie in the window?*

"You want buy what?"

She didn't have much English. The person who did was late showing up for work. "You come again, twelve o'clock maybe, one—"

"No. I want to buy the mannequin . . . the *doll*." They had finally agreed on this word. "Now. For a hundred dollars." He had no idea what store mannequins cost.

She shook her head. "No, I cannot—"

"Two hundred dollars. Cash." He took out his wallet.

They settled on two fifty. She stripped the overalls and blouse off the mannequin, and, to his relief, she put it in a large, opaque suit bag. Ethan watched its stiff plastic form—hairless, with a monochromatic and expressionless face—disappear into the bag. He put it in the trunk of his car, pushing from his mind every bad B-movie about murderers and wrapped-up bodies.

* * *

Marilyn Mahjoub was fifteen minutes late for her first testing session. Waiting, Jamie paced, smacking a fist into his palm, dialing the energy all the way up to ten. "You know, Dr. Stone Man, we'd be so much farther along with Mape if all the fucking subfields of AI research hadn't been—oh, I don't know—slogging along for sixty or seventy years without fucking *communicating* with each other?"

"Yes," Ethan said.

"It's just such a . . . oh, by the way, I changed some of our girl's heuristics. What I did was—are you listening to me? Hello?"

"I'm listening," Ethan said, although he wasn't, not really.

"You're not listening. Mape listens to me more than you do, don't you, Mape?"

"I'm listening," MAIP said.

"Why is she so much more *here* than you are? And why is that kid so late?"

If there was a reason, they never heard it. Marilyn Mahjoub arrived eventually, in the custody of a sullen older brother. Her clothing embodied the culture clash suggested by her name: hijab, tight jeans, and crop top. She had huge dark eyes and a slender, awkward grace. In a few years she would be beautiful.

Like Cassie McAvoy, Marilyn played the keyboard. Unlike Cassie, she was good at it. Ethan could picture her in a concert hall one day, rising to cries of "Brava!" However, she did not take well to MAIP.

"Try playing that last section slower," MAIP said in the warm, pretty voice that Jamie had given her. She was comparing Marilyn's rendition, note by note, to the professional version in memory.

Marilyn's lip curled. "No. It shouldn't be slower."

"Let's try it just to see."

"No! I had it right!"

"You did really well," MAIP said. "Can I please hear the piece again?"

Jamie nodded briskly; MAIP was acting to lower Marilyn's frustration level by offering praise and neutrally suggesting a redo. Ethan studied the data display. Frustration level was not lowering.

"No," Marilyn said, "I won't play it again. I don't *need* to play it again. I did it right already."

"You did really well," MAIP said. "I can see that you're talented."

"Then don't tell me to do it slower!"

"Mare," said her brother, with much disgust, "*chill*."

Jamie stepped in. "What would you like to play now, Marilyn?"

Her childish pique disappeared. Lowering her head, Marilyn looked up at Jamie through her lashes and purred, "What would you like to hear?"

Christ—twelve years old! Were all young girls like this now? Allyson wouldn't have been. She would have been direct, intelligent, appealing.

Jamie, flustered (Ethan hadn't known that was possible), said, "Play. . . uh, what else do you . . . what do you want to play?"

Later, after brother and sister had left, Jamie turned on Ethan. "What's wrong with you?"

"With me?"

"You've been distracted this whole session and you made me deal with that little wildcat by myself! Did you even hear me say that I added heuristics to Mape, matching emotion with postural clues?"

"No, I . . . Yes."

"Uh huh. Get with it, Ethan! We have to get this right!"

Ethan said, "Don't take your frustration with Marilyn out on me."

MAIP said, "Jamie, you seem distressed."

Startled, Ethan turned toward the computer. "MAIP has your data? Did you give your baseline readings to her?"

"No!" Jamie's irritation disappeared, replaced instantly with buoyancy; it was like a dolphin breaking the surface of gray water. "Well, I gave her some data, anyway—but I think she applied the postural heuristics and the other new stuff and . . . I don't know, you'll have to do the analysis, but I think she actually *learned*!"

Ethan gazed at MAIP. A pile of intricate machinery, a complex arrangement of electrons. For some reason he couldn't name, he felt a prickle of fear.

* * *

It was after ten when the last researchers left Building 6. In Building 5, the Biological Division, lights still burned. Perez and Chung clattered out together, talking excitedly. Maybe they'd had another breakthrough, or maybe they just loved their work.

Ethan knew he didn't love his work on MAIP, no more than a castaway loved his raft. Depended on it, was grateful for it, needed it. But love was nowhere anymore, unless it was here.

"Hi, Daddy."

"Hi, baby."

The mannequin from Zhao Tailoring wore one of Allyson's dresses, still hanging in her closet at Ethan's apartment. The mannequin had jointed arms and legs. Ethan carefully positioned it into a sitting position. It was a little too tall for the projection, and he had to wrap the bottom four inches of plastic with his raincoat. That was all right; when he projected Allyson onto the mannequin, it looked as if she had plopped herself down onto his coat. Maybe after playing dress-up, maybe just with five-year-old mischief. Ethan set the lights to low, put the stuffed Piglet into her arms, and added the projected overlays, one by one. Healthy skin, glossy hair, bright eyes.

"Hi, Daddy."

"Hi, baby."

Ethan's knees trembled. Slowly he knelt beside her, the coat buttons lumpy under his calves. Lightly—so lightly, the VR glove on his right hand feeling her skin but not the hard plastic below—he used his left arm to hug his daughter.

"Hi, Daddy."

"What the *fuck*?"

Lights crashed on full; illusion crashed with them. Ethan jumped up. Jamie said, "What the hell are you doing? Laura called me, she saw you go into—"

"Go away. Leave me alone."

He didn't. But Jamie's face, always so confident, turned a mottled maroon of embarrassment. "Hey, man, I'm sorry, I didn't mean to—" Then confusion and embarrassment vanished. "No, I'm not sorry! Ethan, somebody has to level with you. You can't go on like this. I know—we all know—what you've been through. As tough as it gets, yeah. But you have to . . . This isn't *normal*. That model isn't Allyson. You *know* that. You have to let go, move on, accept that she's gone instead of . . . This is a perversion of technology, Ethan. I'm sorry, but that's what it is. And also a perversion of Allyson's mem—"

He didn't finish the sentence. Ethan crossed the floor in a mad dash and knocked him down.

Jamie looked up at Ethan from the floor. He wasn't hurt or even winded; Ethan was no fighter and Jamie outweighed him by at least forty pounds. Ethan had merely pushed him over. Jamie got up, shook his head like a pit bull hurling away a carcass, and left without a word.

Ethan began to tremble.

His fingers shook so much that he could barely shut down the programs. He left the mannequin sitting in the middle of the floor, a lifeless hunk of plastic, and left his coat and the stuffed Piglet with it. He couldn't bear to touch any of them.

Outside, in the dark and blowing rain, there was no sign of Jamie. Ethan lurched to Building 18. He had nowhere else to go. He couldn't drive; he could barely see. The tarry mist was back in his brain, filling it, chilling him to the marrow. There had never been anyplace else to go, not for a year. It frightened him that he couldn't feel the sidewalk beneath his feet, couldn't hear the raindrops strike the ground.

In the AI lab, lights burned and the flight simulator was running. Jamie must have been working late. But Jamie wasn't here now, and if Ethan didn't do something—anything—he would die. That was how he felt—how Tina must have felt. Thinking of Tina only made him feel worse. He stumbled to the game console and squeezed himself into the small chair in front of it. His hands gripped the controls. At least he could feel them, solid under his fingers: the only solid thing in his world of black mist and tarry cold. Black mist as a train sped into Westlake Tunnel Station, as an unseen virus ate into nerve and tissue . . .

"You have just crashed the jet," MAIP said. "Let's try again!"

Train speeding forward at forty miles per hour . . . "Hi, Daddy" . . . keep going keep going don't give in or you'll explode you will be Tina . . . damn bitch how could she leave me like that not my fault Moser's Syndrome not my fault . . . *don't give in* . . .

"You have crashed the jet. But I know you can do this—let's try again!"

Over and over he crashed the jet, even as MAIP made it harder and harder for him to fail. He smashed the jet into mountains, into desert, into the sea. Again and again and again. Someone spoke to him, or didn't. There was noise again, a lot of noise, there was destruction and death as there *should* be, to classify reality, to match the ontology of everything he had lost—

And then, finally, he realized the noise was his own screaming, and he stopped.

Into the silence MAIP said, "You were very angry, Ethan. I hope you feel better now."

He gave a little gasp, first at MAIP's words and then because he wasn't alone. Jamie stood beside him with Laura Avery.

She said gently, "Are you all right?" And when Ethan didn't answer, she added, "Jamie called me. After I called him, I mean. I saw you carrying something into Building 6 and—"

Jamie interrupted. "When did you input your data into MAIP?"

Ethan said nothing. The tarry cold mist had receded. No—it had vanished. He felt limp, drained, bruised, as if he had fallen off a cliff and somehow survived. *You were very angry. I hope you feel better now.*

"You didn't, did you?" Jamie demanded. "You never gave your baseline data to MAIP! She did a cold reading on you, extrapolating from free-form observation! We didn't teach her to do that!"

"Be quiet," Laura said. "Jamie, for God's sake—*not now*."

MAIP said, "Ethan, I'm glad you feel better. You were both angry and sad before. You were sad even when you smiled."

Jamie drew a sharp, whistling breath. "Detection of social pretense! I'm sorry, Ethan, I know you're upset and I said some things I shouldn't have, but—detection of social pretense! From cold readings! She's taken a huge step forward—she *knows* you!"

Ethan said, not to Jamie but to the complexity of machinery and electrons that was MAIP, "You don't know me. You're a nonlinear statistical modeling tool."

Laura said, "But I'm not." She put a tentative hand on his arm.

Jamie said, "Mape's not, either. Not anymore. She *learned*, Ethan. She did!"

Ethan looked at the flight simulator, which flashed the total number of jets he had crashed. He looked at MAIP. He saw the mannequin, a pathetic lump of plastic that he had left in Building 6.

Ethan rose. He had to steady himself with one hand on the game console. Laura's hand on his arm felt warm through his damp shirt. He didn't, he realized, know any of them, not really: not Laura, not MAIP, not Jamie. Not himself. Especially not himself.

He would have to learn everything all over again, reassess everything, forge new algorithms. Starting with this moment, here, now, to the sound of rain on the roof of the building.

Bibliography

Novels and Standalone Novellas

The Prince of Morning Bells, Timescape, 1981.
The Golden Grove, Bluejay, 1984.
The White Pipes, Bluejay, 1985.
An Alien Light, Arbor House, 1988.
Brain Rose, William Morrow, 1990.
Beggars in Spain, Avon, 1993.
Beggars and Choosers, Tor, 1994.
Beggars Ride, Tor, 1996.
Oaths and Miracles, Forge/St. Martin's, 1997.
Stinger, Forge/St. Martin's, 1998.
Maximum Light, Tor, 1998.
Probability Moon, Tor, 2000.
Probability Sun, Tor, 2001.
Probability Space, Tor, 2002.
Nothing Human, Golden Gryphon Press, 2003.
Crossfire, Tor, 2003.
Crucible, Tor, 2004.
Dogs, Tachyon, 2008.
Steal Across the Sky, Tor, 2009.
After the Fall, Before the Fall, During the Fall, Tachyon, 2012.

Yesterday's Kin, Tachyon, 2014.
Tomorrow's Kin, Tor, 2017.
If Tomorrow Comes, Tor, 2018.
Terran Tomorrow, Tor, 2018.
Sea Change, Tachyon, 2020.
The Eleventh Gate, Baen, 2020.
Observer (with Robert Lanza), Story Plant, 2023.

Young Adult Novels

Yanked, Avon, 1999.
Writing as Anna Kendall:
Crossing Over, Gollancz, 2010.
Dark Mist Rising, Gollancz, 2011.
A Bright and Terrible Sword, Indigo, 2012.
Flash Point, Viking, 2012.

Story Collections

Trinity and Other Stories, Bluejay, 1985.
The Aliens of Earth, Arkham House, 1993.
Beaker's Dozen, Tor, 1998.
Nano Comes to Clifford Falls and Other Stories, Golden Gryphon Press, 2008.
Fountain of Age: Stories, Small Beer Press, 2012.
The Best of Nancy Kress, Subterranean Press, 2015.

Nonfiction Books on Writing

Beginnings, Middles, and Ends, Writers Digest Books, 1993.
Dynamic Characters, Writers Digest Books, 1998.
Character, Emotion, and Viewpoint, Writers Digest Books, 2004.

As Editor

Nebula Awards Showcase 2003, New American Library, 2003.

Short Fiction (first appearance only)

"The Earth Dwellers," *Galaxy*, December 1976.
"A Delicate Shade of Kipney," *Isaac Asimov's Science Fiction*, January–February 1978.
"And Whether Pigs Have Wings," *Omni*, January 1979.
"Against a Crooked Stile," *Isaac Asimov's Science Fiction,* May 1979.
"Shadows on the Cave Wall," *Universe 11*, Doubleday, 1981.
"Green Thumb," *Terrors*, Berkley, 1982.
"With the Original Cast," *Omni*, May 1982.
"A Little Matter of Timing," *Fantasy & Science Fiction*, September 1982.
"Talp Hunt," *Universe 12*, Doubleday,1982.
"Night Win," *Isaac Asimov's Science Fiction*, September 1983.
"Borovsky's Hollow Woman" (with Jeff Duntemann), *Omni*, October 1983.
"Explanations, Inc.," *Fantasy & Science Fiction*, July 1984.
"Ten Thousand Pictures, One Word," *Twilight Zone*, August 1984.
"Trinity," *Isaac Asimov's Science Fiction*, October 1984.
"Birth Luck," *Liavek*, Ace Books, 1985.
"Out of All Them Bright Stars," *Fantasy & Science Fiction*, March 1985.
"Down Behind Cuba Lake," *Isaac Asimov's Science Fiction,* August 1986.
"Phone Repairs," *Isaac Asimov's Science Fiction*, December 1986.
"Training Ground," *Liavek: Wizard's Row*, Ace Books, 1987.
"Cannibals," *Isaac Asimov's Science Fiction*, May 1987.
"Glass," *Isaac Asimov's Science Fiction*, September 1987.
"Philippa's Hands," *Full Spectrum*, Bantam Spectra, 1988.
"Craps," *Isaac Asimov's Science Fiction*, March 1988.
"Spillage," *Fantasy & Science Fiction*, April 1988.

"In Memoriam," *Isaac Asimov's Science Fiction*, June 1988.
"In a World Like This," *Omni*, October 1988.
"The Price of Oranges," *Isaac Asimov's Science Fiction,* April 1989.
"People Like Us," *Isaac Asimov's Science Fiction*, September 1989.
"Renaissance," *Isaac Asimov's Science Fiction*, December 1989.
"Inertia," *Analog*, January 1990.
"Touchdown," *Isaac Asimov's Science Fiction*, October 1990.
"Peace of Mind," *When the Music's Over*, Bantam Spectra, 1991.
"Beggars in Spain," Axolotl Press, 1991, and *Isaac Asimov's Science Fiction*, April 1991.
"And Wild for to Hold," *Isaac Asimov's Science Fiction*, July 1991.
"The Mountain to Mohammed," *Isaac Asimov's Science Fiction,* April 1992.
"Birthing Pool," *Murasaki*, Bantam, 1992.
"Eoghan," *Alternate Kennedys*, Tor, 1992.
"To Scale," *Xanadu*, Tor, 1993.
"Stalking Beans," *Snow White, Blood Red*, Avon, 1993.
"The Death of John Patrick Yoder," *Full Spectrum IV*, Bantam, 1993.
"The Battle of Long Island," *Omni*, February 1993.
"Martin on a Wednesday," *Isaac Asimov's Science Fiction,* March 1993.
"Dancing on Air," *Isaac Asimov's Science Fiction*, July 1993.
"Grant Us This Day," *Isaac Asimov's Science Fiction,* September 1993.
"Ars Longa," *Alternate Celebrities*, Bantam, 1994.
"Words Like Pale Stones," *Black Thorn, White Rose*, Avon, 1994.
"Margin of Error," *Omni*, October 1994.
"Summer Wind," *Ruby Slippers, Golden Tears*, Avon, 1995.
"Fault Lines," *Isaac Asimov's Science Fiction*, August 1995.
"Evolution," *Isaac Asimov's Science Fiction*, October 1995.
"Unto the Daughters," *Sisters in Fantasy*, Roc, 1995.

"Feigenbaum Number," *Omni*, December 1995.
"Hard Drive," *Killing Me Softly*, HarperPrism, 1995.
"Sex Education," *Intersections: The Sycamore Hill Anthology*, Tor, 1996.
"Marigold Outlet," *Cat Tails*, Avon, 1996.
"The Flowers of Aulit Prison," *Isaac Asimov's Science Fiction*, October–November 1996.
"Steadfast," *Black Swan, White Raven*, Avon, 1997.
"Always True to Thee, in My Fashion," *Isaac Asimov's Science Fiction*, January 1997.
"Steamship Soldiers on the Information Front," *Future Histories*, Horizon House, 1997.
"A Scientific Education," *Crime Through Time*, Berkley, 1998.
"State of Nature," *Bending the Landscape*, White Wolf Books, 1998.
"Clad in Gossamer," *Silver Birch, Blood Moon*, Avon, 1999.
"Sleeping Dogs," *Far Horizons*, Avon, 1999.
"Savior," *Isaac Asimov's Science Fiction*, June 2000.
"To Cuddle Amy," *Isaac Asimov's Science Fiction*, August 2000.
"Wetlands Preserve," SciFi.com, October 2000.
"My Mother, Dancing," *Isaac Asimov's Science Fiction*, June 2004.
"Computer Virus," *Isaac Asimov's Science Fiction*, April 2001.
"Plant Engineering," *Death Dines at 8:30*, Berkley, 2001.
". . . And No Such Things Grow Here," *Isaac Asimov's Science Fiction,* June 2001.
"Patent Infringement," *Isaac Asimov's Science Fiction*, May 2002.
"The Most Famous Little Girl in the World," SciFi.com, 2003.
"The War on Treemon," *Isaac Asimov's Science Fiction*, January 2003.
"Ej-Es," *Stars*, DAW, 2003.
"Dancing in the Dark," *Space, Inc.*, DAW, 2003.
"Shiva in Shadow," *Between Worlds*, 2004.

"Mirror Image," *One Million A.D.*, DAW, 2005.
"Product Development," *Nature*, March 16, 2006.
"First Flight," *Space Cadets*, 2006.
"Nano Comes to Clifford Falls," *Isaac Asimov's Science Fiction*, July, 2006.
"JQ211F, and Holding," *Forbidden Planets*, SFBC, 2006.
"Solomon's Choice" (with Mike Resnick), *Fast Forward* 1, Pyr, 2007.
"Safeguard," *Isaac Asimov's Science Fiction*, January 2007.
"End Game," *Isaac Asimov's Science Fiction*, April–May 2007.
"Stone Man," *Wizards*, Berkley, 2007.
"Art of War," *The New Space Opera*, HarperCollins, 2007.
"Fountain of Age," *Isaac Asimov's Science Fiction*, July 2007.
"By Fools Like Me," *Isaac Asimov's Science Fiction,* September 2007.
"Laws of Survival," *Jim Baen's Universe*, December 2007.
"The Rules," *Isaac Asimov's Science Fiction*, December 2007.
"Sex and Violence," *Isaac Asimov's Science Fiction*, February 2008.
"Call Back Yesterday," *Isaac Asimov's Science Fiction*, June 2008.
"First Rites," *Jim Baen's Universe*, October 2008.
"The Erdmann Nexus," *Isaac Asimov's Science Fiction*, October 2008.
"The Kindness of Strangers," *Fast Forward*, Pyr, 2009.
"Elevator," *Eclipse 2*, Night Shade Books, 2009.
"Unintended Behavior," *Isaac Asimov's Science Fiction*, January 2009.
"Act One," *Isaac Asimov's Science Fiction*, March 2009.
"Exegesis," *Isaac Asimov's Science Fiction*, April–May 2009.
"Images of Anna," *Fantasy Magazine*, September 2009.
"Deadly Sins," *Isaac Asimov's Science Fiction*, October 2009.
"First Principle," *Life on Mars: Tales from a New Frontier*, Viking, 2011.

"Eliot Wrote," Lightspeed.com, May 2011.
"A Hundred Hundred Daisies," *Isaac Asimov's Science Fiction*, October 2011.
"We Can Do This," *Arc 1.4*, December 2012.
"Writer's Block," *Rip Off!*, Audio Frontiers (audiobook), 2012.
"Knotweed and Gardenias," *Starship Century: Toward the Grand Horizon*, Fairwood Press, 2013.
"Migration," *Beyond the Sun*, Solaris, 2013.
"Mithridates, He Died Old," *Isaac Asimov's Science Fiction*, January 2013.
"More," *Solaris Rising 2*, 2013.
"One," Tor.com, July 2013.
"And Other Stories . . ." *Shadows of the New Sun: Stories in Honor of Gene Wolfe*, Tor, 2013.
"Pathways," *12 Tomorrows*, MIT Tech Review, 2013.
"Annabel Lee," *New Under the Sun*, Phoenix Pick, 2013.
"Frog Watch," *Isaac Asimov's Science Fiction*, December 2013.
"Second Arabesque, Very Slowly," *Dangerous Women*, Tor, 2013.
"The Common Good," *Isaac Asimov's Science Fiction*, January 2014.
"Pretty Soon the Four Horsemen Are Going to Come Riding Through," *The End Is Nigh*, Broad Reach Press, 2014.
"Do You Remember Michael Jones?," *Galaxy's Edge*, May 2014.
"Eaters," *The Book of Silverberg: Stories in Honor of Robert Silverberg*, Subterranean Press, 2014.
"Outmoded Things," *Multiverse: Exploring Poul Anderson's Worlds*, Subterranean Press, 2014.
"Sidewalk at 12:10 P.M.," *Isaac Asimov's Science Fiction*, June 2014.
"Someone to Watch Over Me," *IEE Spectrum*, June 2014.
"Angels of the Apocalypse," *The End Is Now*, Broad Reach Press, 2014.

"Blessings," *The End Has Come*, Broad Reach Press, 2015.
"Cocoons," *Meeting Infinity*, Solaris, 2015.
"Machine Learning," *Future Visions: Original Science Fiction Inspired by Microsoft*, Microsoft, 2015.
"Belief," *Fantasy and Science Fiction*, March–April 2016.
"Pyramid," *Now We Are Ten*, Newcon Press, 2016.
"Every Hour of Light and Dark," *Omni*, Winter 2017.
"Collapse," *Seat 14-C*, X-Prize, 2017.
"Canoe," *Extrasolar*, PS Publishing, 2017.
"Dear Sarah," *Infinity Wars*, Solaris, 2017.
"Ma Ganga," *Technology in 2050*, Profile Books, 2018.
"Cost of Doing Business," *Asimov's Science Fiction*, May–June 2018.
"Semper Augustus," *Asimov's Science Fiction*, March–April 2020.
"Invisible People," *Entanglements*, MIT Press, 2020.
"Little Animals," Clarkesworld.com, June 2021.
"The Alice Run," Reactor.com, August 2024.
"Quantum Ghosts," serialized in *Asimov's Science Fiction*, April–May and June–July 2025.
"The Meaning We Seek," *Lightspeed*, May 2025.

MIDDLE-GRADE STORIES

In the Young Explorer's Adventure Guide series
(Dreaming Robot Press):

"Why I Hate Earth, 2015.
"The Aliens and Me," 2015.
"The Robot Did It," 2016.
"The Great Broccoli Wi-Fi Theft," 2017.

AWARDS

Nebula, Best Short Story 1986, "Out of All Them Bright Stars."
Nebula, Best Novella 1991, "Beggars in Spain."

Hugo, Best Novella 1992, "Beggars in Spain."
Sturgeon Award, Best Short Science Fiction 1997, "The Flowers of Aulit Prison."
Nebula, Best Novelette 1998, "The Flowers of Aulit Prison."
John W. Campbell Memorial Award, Best Novel 2003, *Probability Space.*
Nebula, Best Novella 2007, "Fountain of Age."
Hugo, Best Novella 2009, "The Erdmann Nexus."
Nebula, Best Novella 2012, *After the Fall, Before the Fall, During the Fall.*
Locus Award, Best Novella 2013, *After the Fall, Before the Fall, During the Fall.*
Nebula, Best Novella 2014, *Yesterday's Kin.*
Locus Award, Best Novella 2014, *Yesterday's Kin.*

About the Author

NANCY KRESS IS THE AUTHOR of twenty-seven novels, three books on writing, four short story collections, and over a hundred works of short fiction. Her fiction has won six Nebula Awards, two Hugo Awards, a Sturgeon Award, and a John W. Campbell Memorial Award. Her work has been translated into Swedish, French, Italian, German, Spanish, Danish, Polish, Croatian, Korean, Lithuanian, Chinese, Romanian, Japanese, Russian, and Klingon, none of which she can read.

FRIENDS OF PM

These are indisputably momentous times—the financial system is melting down globally and the Empire is stumbling. Now more than ever there is a vital need for radical ideas.

In the years since its founding—and on a mere shoestring—PM Press has risen to the formidable challenge of publishing and distributing knowledge and entertainment for the struggles ahead. With hundreds of releases to date, we have published an impressive and stimulating array of literature, art, music, politics, and culture. Using every available medium, we've succeeded in connecting those hungry for ideas and information to those putting them into practice.

Friends of PM allows you to directly help impact, amplify, and revitalize the discourse and actions of radical writers, filmmakers, and artists. It provides us with a stable foundation from which we can build upon our early successes and provides a much-needed subsidy for the materials that can't necessarily pay their own way. You can help make that happen—and receive every new title automatically delivered to your door once a month—by joining as a Friend of PM Press. And, we'll throw in a free T-shirt when you sign up.

Here are your options:

- $30 a month: Get all books and pamphlets plus 50% discount on all webstore purchases
- $40 a month: Get all PM Press releases (including CDs and DVDs) plus 50% discount on all webstore purchases
- $100 a month: Superstar—Everything plus PM merchandise, free downloads, and 50% discount on all webstore purchases

For those who can't afford $30 or more a month, we have Sustainer Rates at $15, $10, and $5. Sustainers get a free PM Press T-shirt and a 50% discount on all purchases from our website.

Your Visa or Mastercard will be billed once a month, until you tell us to stop. Or until our efforts succeed in bringing the revolution around. Or the financial meltdown of Capital makes plastic redundant. Whichever comes first.

PM Press is an independent, radical publisher of critically necessary books for our tumultuous times. Our aim is to deliver bold political ideas and vital stories to all walks of life and arm the dreamers to demand the impossible. Founded in 2007 by a small group of people with decades of publishing, media, and organizing experience, we have sold millions of copies of our books, most often one at a time, face to face. We're old enough to know what we're doing and young enough to know what's at stake. Join us to create a better world.

PM Press
PO Box 23912
Oakland, CA 94623
info@pmpress.org

PM Press in Europe
europe@pmpress.org
www.pmpress.org.uk

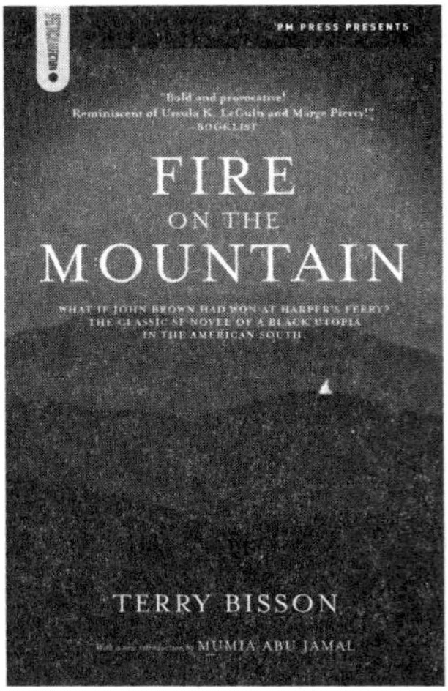

Fire on the Mountain

Terry Bisson
Introduction by Mumia Abu-Jamal
ISBN: 978-1-60486-087-0
208 pages • 5 x 8 • $18.95

It's 1959 in socialist Virginia. The Deep South is an independent Black nation called Nova Africa. The second Mars expedition is about to touch down on the red planet. And a pregnant scientist is climbing the Blue Ridge in search of her great-great grandfather, a teenage slave who fought with John Brown and Harriet Tubman's guerrilla army.

Long unavailable in the U.S., published in France as *Nova Africa*, *Fire on the Mountain* is the story of what might have happened if John Brown's raid on Harper's Ferry had succeeded—and the Civil War had been started not by the slave owners but the abolitionists.

"History revisioned, turned inside out . . . Bisson's wild and wonderful imagination has taken some strange turns to arrive at such a destination."
—Madison Smartt Bell, Anisfield-Wolf Award winner and author of *Devil's Dream*

TERRY BISSON
THE LEFT LEFT BEHIND
KIM STANLEY ROBINSON
THE LUCKY STRIKE
ELEANOR ARNASON
MAMMOTHS OF THE GREAT PLAINS
GARY PHILLIPS
THE UNDERBELLY
MICHAEL MOORCOCK
MODEM TIMES 2.0
URSULA K. LE GUIN
THE WILD GIRLS
CORY DOCTOROW
THE GREAT BIG BEAUTIFUL TOMORROW
RUDY RUCKER
SURFING THE GNARL
NALO HOPKINSON
REPORT FROM PLANET MIDNIGHT
KEN MACLEOD
THE HUMAN FRONT
JOHN SHIRLEY
NEW TABOOS
KAREN JOY FOWLER
THE SCIENCE OF HERSELF
NORMAN SPINRAD
RAISING HELL
PAUL KRASSNER
PATTY HEARST & THE TWINKIE MURDERS: A TALE OF TWO TRIALS
MARGE PIERCY
MY LIFE, MY BODY
CARTER SCHOLZ
GYPSY

OUTSPOKEN AUTHORS